PENGUIN BOOKS

THE GIRL
FROM THE SEA

James Aldridge grew up in Swan Hill in Victoria, Australia.
In 1938, he moved to London where he established a career in
journalism, working for major international news publications.
The Organisation of International Journalists awarded him the
gold medal for journalism in 1972.

James Aldridge has written about thirty novels for adults and
children, short stories, plays, non-fiction, television scripts and
journalism. His writing has been published in forty languages.

James Aldridge is probably best known in Australia for his
novels set in the fictional town of St Helen during the Depres-
sion of the 1930s. These novels are as loved by adults as they
are by children. They include *Ride a Wild Pony* (adapted for the
screen by Walt Disney), *My Brother Tom* (made into a TV
series), *The True Story of Spit MacPhee* (also adapted for television plus winner of the 1986 New South Wales Premier's
Literary Award and the 1986 *Guardian* Award), *The True Story
of Lilli Stubeck* (1985 CBCA Book of the Year) and *The True
Story of Lola Mackellar*.

'A dazzling story . . . none who reads it will forget it.'
Australian Bookseller & Publisher

THE GIRL
FROM THE SEA

JAMES
ALDRIDGE

PENGUIN BOOKS

Penguin Books

Published by the Penguin Group
Penguin Books Australia Ltd
250 Camberwell Road,
Camberwell, Victoria 3124, Australia
Penguin Books Ltd
80 Strand, London WC2R 0RL, England
Penguin Putnam Inc.
375 Hudson Street, New York, New York 10014, USA
Penguin Books, a division of Pearson Canada
10 Alcorn Avenue, Toronto, Ontario, Canada, M4V 3B2
Penguin Books (N.Z.) Ltd
Cnr Rosedale and Airborne Roads, Albany, Auckland, New Zealand
Penguin Books (South Africa) (Pty) Ltd
24 Sturdee Avenue, Rosebank, Johannesburg 2196, South Africa
Penguin Books India (P) Ltd
11, Community Centre, Panchsheel Park, New Delhi 110 017, India

First published by Penguin Books Australia, 2002

3 5 7 9 10 8 6 4

Cover design by Jo Hunt
Text design by Karen Trump, Penguin Design Studio
Typeset in 11/16 pt Berkeley by Midland Typesetters, Maryborough, Victoria
Printed and bound in Australia by McPherson's Printing Group,
Maryborough, Victoria

Cataloguing-in-Publication data for this book is available from
the National Library of Australia

ISBN 0 14 300112 4.

www.penguin.com.au

PROLOGUE

I'm not sure how I can tell the real story of the Provençal girl I knew as Lelée, back in the 1950s. I know so much more about her now than I did when she literally burst from the sea under my dinghy, emerging like a samite thing from the blue lagoon of the Bay of Angels at Villefranche-sur-Mer. But, looking back on it, I suppose that an organised sort of hindsight is the best way to explain what happened in those distant days in the South of France before the beautiful Midi was taken over by the rest of Europe.

Originally, it was the English and Russian aristocracy who fashioned the coast into an indulgent and enchanting winter resort when they occupied the Midi over a hundred

1

years ago. Queen Victoria was a regular visitor, usually with a hundred servants. The memory of that bygone age is still present in the palatial villas, luxurious hotels and gambling casinos they built. But not the beaches. That came later, after the First World War. It was the rich Americans who transformed the coast into a summer resort, which also attracted the European middle classes. Only in the aftermath of the Second World War did the masses of the north and elsewhere arrive to spend their two weeks' summer holidays in the sun and sea and on organised beaches. That was about to happen when I was there. The topless age had not yet arrived, but the beaches were full, and they became an important part of Lelée's life.

Though she was thirteen at the time, the same age as I was, she had already been arrested at sea with her father as a smuggler. Mediterranean smuggling now is not what it used to be. The traditional kind of smuggling I'm talking about in the 1950s was nothing to do with drugs. In those days it was either big boats dumping large sealed crates of whisky or cigarettes way off shore, or it was a local in-shore sideline for some of the Provençal fishermen who had always considered the Mediterranean coast from Menton to Marseilles a private right-of-way for whatever they wanted to do with it.

In fact smuggling along the Mediterranean coast of France had a long history. A hundred and fifty years ago it had almost become an accepted if illegal business. In those days untaxed goods were smuggled into one port or another, and the business then was in fabrics, silks, spices, tobacco and spirits. What changed all that was war-time smuggling when tartanes, small boats, smuggled almost anything in short supply because of the war. Avoiding Customs in the 1900s meant hiding the stuff in hidden coves and small inlets, but when that became too risky smugglers began to use the sea itself as the best place to dump and hide the contraband.

The miseries of the Second World War gave this kind of smuggling a new incentive, particularly when it became possible to encase almost anything in waterproof vinyl or plastics. Smugglers could sink anything anywhere along the coast, with only a lobster-pot marker to indicate where it was and deceive the Customs. And that was how it came into the domain of the Provençal fishermen of the Midi in the '50s when I was there.

Smuggling meant a supplement to their meagre income from the nets, lobster pots and fish traps. Some of the fishermen also enjoyed the danger and the challenge of it and, as it happened, Lelée's blind courage was obviously a heritage from her fisherman father, known as 'Lou Rabo Lelée', or 'the long radish Lelée', which was his Provençal name. But Lou Rabo was better known to his Provençal compatriots as 'Lou Corsairo Rabo', or simply 'the Corsairo' – 'the Buccaneer' – which was a fair description of what he was – a dare-devil of the sea.

From the age of six Lelée had been at sea with her father, fishing and later diving for him. At the age of ten she had been arrested with the Corsairo when they were lifting lobster pots off Cap Mal – lobster pots with smuggled containers of Swiss watches. By then she had become his underwater troubleshooter who could do anything for him at any depth up to ten feet, allowing for her lung size and her age.

When arrested with her father she had been taken off in a blue van to the Marine Gendarmerie at Fréjus, and because the Corsairo had a temperament to fit his reputation, he didn't think of his arrest (the fourth) as anything but a bad-luck interruption to his normal life, and he would gladly engage himself to anyone who was willing to enjoy it with him. The gendarmes were willing and he bavarded with them all the way to their headquarters in Fréjus.

Lelée herself wasn't charged with her father. Being ten at the time she was sent home to her English mother in Saint-Jean-Cap-Ferrat, the little town we all knew simply as Saint Jean. The Corsairo was given two months in La Baumette prison in Marseilles for 'complicité', against which he protested loudly to the court that he could swear, as God was his personal judge, that he thought his lobster pots had been full of things with claws, not things with Swiss wheels. 'In any case,' he added, 'my daughter is as innocent as a fish, so you're not going to confuse her with me.'

Lelée objected. 'I'm not a fish,' she told the court. 'I'm his daughter, and I'm a girl.'

The judge-of-instruction knew the Corsairo's family and it was he who sent Lelée home. But the next time Lelée was caught she was on her own, searching for an underwater cave near Cap Roux where Italian contrabandists had stashed a complete Vespa motor scooter sealed in a big vinyl sack. It was hidden in one of the underwater caves off the Cap, and the Corsairo had sent Lelée by bus to see if she could identify it from the road. She could only find it from the sea, but even in the sea she couldn't dive deep enough to find

4

the Vespa because her eleven-year-old lungs couldn't take in enough air to reach the cave.

Unfortunately the Customs men had been stalking her and watching her. They apparently knew that the Vespa was there, and this time she was charged as a minor in need of care and protection. She had to appear in a French version of a Children's Court, and though she was once again given in care of her mother, she was warned that it would mean custodial detention if she was ever caught again; moreover her mother too would be charged with wilful neglect.

Lelée's mother was an Englishwoman, but she was also a Provençal fisherman's wife who had been easily conquered by the Corsairo, although it had soon become a conquest of equals because she had as much confidence in the world as the Corsairo himself. She was, in fact, the original model for Lelée; or rather mother, daughter, husband and wife were all of the same temperament. Originally she had come to France almost by accident. She had been working for an English family named Caldwell as their children's watchdog, and when they had spent some time on Cap Ferrat with friends, the Caldwells had simply taken off one day in their hosts' yacht, leaving their watchdog to fend for herself in Saint Jean.

Irrepressible in any world she was left with, she had found work in an artists' colony set up by a wealthy Englishwoman in a villa on the Cap called The Spaniards. She had become a weaver, and she had been a frequent visitor to the shop run by the Corsairo's mother in Saint Jean for the raw bolts of linen and other stuff used by local Provençal weavers for their own kind of work. Being a stray, and an orphan, it *wasn't difficult for this English girl to overcome the differences between herself and the attentive Corsairo. Barriers were not her problem, and in the end she had abandoned her weaving to marry the Corsairo, Rabo Lelée, and thereafter she was known locally with a special emphasis for her uniqueness as the Rabetto Maero which was the Provençal version of her name, Mireille or Mirella.*

The Rabetto had not only abandoned her weaving, she had been taken over by the fishermen's wives in Saint Jean who thrived on their Provençal bravura. Despite their own verbal contests and rivalries, they had decided that this young Anglaise needed their protection, even though she was as rational, or irrational, as they were. In the end only her English face and English skin and English eyes separated her from these Provençal women in black who tended the nets and fed their husbands. If she was soon able to speak their local Provençal dialect fluently it was really her skill with the nets that persuaded them to accept her. As a weaver she was able, after a few short lessons, to be as fast and as sure in repairing the nets as the women who were born to it and had worked at it all their lives.

When Lelée was born, there was plenty of local regret that she wasn't a boy, because boys became the hard-working back-breakers and girls became the net-menders. But Lelée would soon prove that she was more than equal to any boy so that her devoted father had treated her as a boy, if only because she had his character as well as her mother's. So Lelée became the 'fillou-Corsairo' – the 'girl Corsairo' who soon learned to live by her own rules, fishing or smuggling, but with a devotion to her mother that was only equalled by her father's. In fact her mother, the Rabetto, had never interfered with Lelée's upbringing as a fisherman's 'son', not even in the extremes of the Corsairo's smuggling. But she did insist that Lelée spoke English with her, which was no effort for Lelée who was a natural linguist.

Finally, when the Corsairo's boat was rammed and sunk inadvertently one night by a Customs' patrol launch, and he hadn't returned and never would from his usual midnight exchanges at sea, it began a new life for Lelée and her mother who were forced now to provide for themselves. In the end the Rabetto went back to her weaving, and for her luck the Englishwoman who had originally organised the artists' colony still owned The Spaniards villa on the hill. She gave the Rabetto the gardener's old cottage, where the hand looms had been stored after the colony had been abandoned the year before. From there she and Lelée set up their life without the Corsairo, selling the cloth the Rabetto made for the new shops opening up in Saint Jean but mainly to the tourists who came to the beaches in Beaulieu and Villefranche. It was Lelée who did the bargaining and selling, preferably for foreign currency which, she said, was more reliable than French money.

That was the situation Lelée, aged thirteen, and her mother were in when I came into their lives. Though I was a normal thirteen-year-old English boy, I was a bit of a physical wreck.

Both my father and I had been badly injured in an explosion which shouldn't have happened. My father was a physicist who had become an expert in the peaceful application of explosives, not the chemistry of explosions but their physical behaviour. In fact he knew, scientifically, what an explosion would do, even to the point of making an exact calculation of what would result from any explosion, big or small, although constructively he was mostly concerned with very large explosions.

The accident had happened when he had taken me to a village in Cornwall on the south-west coast of England to see a sea trench for a pipeline being 'dug' by a series of twelve explosions, each a minute apart. It was a spectacular display of exploding water, sand and rock. One by one the explosions worked perfectly until the last of them which turned out to be a colossal freak. It blew up like a huge bomb, sending a small but powerful tidal wave into the remnants of the little stone cottage where we were sheltering. It not only crushed the solid stone walls but we were buried under the rubble as the walls came down. The explosion wasn't the result of my father's perfect system, it was caused by faults in the geological survey which had failed to detect or reveal the tunnels of an old mine which were still intact but filled with natural methane gas. It was the gas that had caused the big explosion, and the result was disastrous for my father and me.

He lost his left eye and his lower left arm, and his spine was badly damaged though not broken. He was unconscious for seven weeks. I lost my sight and was paralysed from the waist down. Six months in and out of hospitals for both of us, and then three months more for therapy and rehabilitation had left me with half-functioning legs and very little eyesight, both of which would eventually repair themselves, the experts said. My father had more or less recovered his stability, though minus half an arm and one eye, but I was still unable to walk or see properly without powerful spectacles. Worse – I was cursed with a fear of anything unexpected, so I was over-cautious to the point of being reluctant to do anything I couldn't see or do properly. I think this was really fear that a false step could cause another disaster, so I still stumbled and groped and did my best to overcome my nerves.

At the end of a miserable nine months of a long, dark winter, my indomitable but untouchable French mother was exhausted by the exacting work tending and nursing and protecting my father and me. It was May and she had finally, for relief, sent me and my eight-year-old sister, Fanny, to spend the summer with her Aunt Mimi who lived on Cap Ferrat, a few miles from Saint Jean, at the other end of the peninsula. Aunt Mimi was a rich and rather eccentric widow, originally from Brittany, but more importantly she was one of those women who had no barriers for good order or right or wrong except her own interpretation for any of it. I know now that my mother, who was also a Bretonne and unconventional, put her trust in Aunt Mimi's systems of behaviour and authority to help me out of my condition, whatever her peculiarities. She was convinced that it would be Aunt Mimi's way, rather than the various doctors and experts and behavioural psychologists, that would rescue me from my problems.

And that is when I first met Lelée.

CHAPTER 1

When Lelée emerged that day from the sea, like a nymph from the depths, pushing off the dinghy with her feet and cursing in a strange language, I was more surprised than scared, but there was worse to come.

It had been a difficult day anyway. Since arriving at Cap Ferrat in the late spring I had spent the first two days at Aunt Mimi's confined to the little pebbly beach which my father had originally created for her with a couple of clever explosions into the cliff face below her villa. The explosions had given Aunt Mimi a perfect inlet of her own. But that had been three years ago. This time, with my helpless legs and eyes, I had spent those first days sitting on the edge of the stony beach reading with difficulty and regretting that I could no longer plunge into the bay and swim to the horizon as I used to. Two days like that became too much for Aunt Mimi who said to me, 'Can you row a dinghy?', to which I replied, 'Of course I can.' So Aunt Mimi told me with the Breton emphasis which had more force than persuasion in it, 'Then you must do it and row it. It is all there waiting for you. I had Ibrahim get it ready for you, so get in it and row it out to sea.' Ibrahim was an elderly Algerian in Saint Jean whom Aunt Mimi depended on when she needed a man's help.

When Aunt Mimi created an order she had to be obeyed, so refusing walking sticks but with Fanny's help, I got down the stairs and tumbled into the dinghy which was moored to the private walk-way attached to the Boat House. I was mostly helpless from the waist down and because of my bad eyesight I told Fanny to undo the painter and sit in the bow, making sure I didn't hit the rocks as I began to manipulate the oars.

'Don't go too fast and it won't matter if you do hit the rocks,' she said. Fanny was already my source of feminine strength, and I knew that my mother had told her to watch over me, which she enjoyed doing, aged eight, because watching over someone was going to be her natural and forceful role in life.

The dinghy was flat-bottomed, and typical of the runner boats, the *coureur barquettes* the fishermen used with their fishing vessels, the *pointus*. But though it was long-nosed and heavy I was surprised how easy it was to row the dinghy and I told Fanny I would keep close to the cliff face looking for the underwater caves I remembered when I had done this with my father.

'Don't get too close,' Fanny shouted again as I began to row along the indented coastline facing the Bay of Angels.

There were no public beaches here, only slopes running down to the bay. On top were the old houses of the rich, including Aunt Mimi's villa. But I still remember the shadows in the rocks that might have been caves, and I bumped along the sides of the Cap until I came to the big fracture near the Phare, the lighthouse on the Pointe Malalongue.

I was leaning over the side, trying to peer through my spectacles into a mysterious gash in the edge of the cliff that disappeared into the depths, when the girl's head suddenly burst from the sea and with what I know now to be a litany of Provençal insults, she pushed the dinghy with such force that we went clear away from the shore. She kept pushing us into the bay, shouting in French, '*Va t'en. Va t'en.*' Which was her way of saying 'Clear off.' Then she disappeared underwater again as if by nature that was where she had come from and was going back to, but not before Fanny had shouted at her, 'You're mad,' and I too had yelled my head off.

Though the girl seemed to have disappeared I didn't know what she would do next so I decided to get out of the way. I turned and fled the place in shameful retreat.

'You shouldn't have done that,' Fanny said angrily.

'I know,' I told her, 'but I'm helpless, Fan.'

By the next day I had managed to overcome my shame and, recovering some of my common sense, and again with Fanny's help, I got down the steps to the Boat House and this time, rowing along the cliffs, I kept twisting around to be sure that the girl from the sea wouldn't surprise us again when I reached Pointe Malalongue where the Phare was.

'What was she doing there anyway?' Fanny kept saying.

'She must be hiding something,' I said.

'Next time she'll probably tip the dinghy right over,' Fanny said, 'and you know I can't swim very well.'

'She can't do that,' I said 'It's too flat and heavy.'

'She looked mad enough to do anything, so don't go too close.'

'I'm just going to take a look,' I told her.

Because I was trying to keep a sharp look-out behind me it became too difficult to row, so I turned my body around and sculled the dinghy which meant that I could see ahead. Out in the bay I could hear music from a cruise ship, by which time I was at the opening of the underwater gash which had a silvery sort of clarity in it, as if there was light in the cave from somewhere else.

I wondered if it were possible to see inside that deep cut without getting into the water, so I looked around cautiously and then crouched down to lean over the side of the dinghy to get closer. But even as I did so the girl's head and arms suddenly burst from the sea again. This time she pulled herself up out of the water in front of us and snatched off my spectacles. She shouted something and then threw them far out into the bay, leaving me virtually blind.

For a moment I groped around in the dinghy looking for my spectacles because I had not seen her pitching them into the sea. 'Where are they? What did she do with them?' I said in a panic to Fanny.

'She must be crazy,' Fanny shouted. 'She threw them way off into the bay.'

'Show me where,' I said, returning to the rowing seat and groping now for the oars in the obscure darkness of my poor sight.

'What's the point?' Fanny said. 'They're gone.'

'They might float . . .'

'No, they won't,' Fanny said, but under her instructions I manoeuvred the dinghy to reach the place where she thought the spectacles had disappeared. I groped around in the water as Fanny held my shirt. She screamed as the girl's head appeared again. This time the girl came right up over the dinghy, took a quick look at my face and, seeing the scars around my eyes, said, '*Oh, mon Dieu, mon Dieu*,' and disappeared again.

'What did she do that for?' Fanny was shouting. 'What's the matter with her?'

'Never mind that,' I said and told her to guide me back along the side of the bay, bumping into the cliff face as she said 'right' or 'left' until finally we reached the Boat House. I shipped the oars and groped for the painter so that Fanny could hold the dinghy while I somehow got onto the wooden laths of the walk-way. Then I began to pull the dinghy laboriously into the covered Boat House.

'You'll slip,' Fanny told me.

'I'm all right,' I said. Though I was still shaking like a leaf I had to re-establish myself with Fanny.

'We can leave the dinghy out here,' Fanny said.

'I don't trust that girl,' I replied and told her to help me close the big doors. 'I'll take one side and you take the other.'

Fanny said that she should run upstairs to get my spare spectacles but I insisted. 'Get me to the stairs and I'll be all right,' I told her irritably.

'But it's too dark in here even for me.'

'You just walk ahead of me.'

'I can't see.'

'Do it, Fan. You can do it.'

'I told you that girl was mad,' she said as I put my hand on her shoulder and manipulated my useless legs to reach the wooden stairs. I pulled myself to the top where the door opened up to the long corridor that became the house above.

CHAPTER 2

Strictly speaking the Boat House was more than a boat house. Originally, the aluminium structure on the sea below the villa had been built by Uncle Theophile, Aunt Mimi's husband, to house his boats. But when Uncle Theophile had given up his long life, Aunt Mimi had been too lonely in the big villa on the hill, so she had rented it out to foreigners while she lived in the comfortable six-roomed villa built to her requirements and sitting on the water above the original boat house. Now it was all one and the same place we called the Boat House.

My mother's last word to Fanny and me as she saw us off from London for the Nice airport, with tickets sent by

Aunt Mimi, and an air hostess holding on to me, were, 'You must obey your Aunt Mimi, even when she seems odd. You know what she's like, but she will help you, Beau, and that's what I'm counting on. You listen to her and do what she wants. And you're not to make things difficult for her, although with Aunt Mimi that's unlikely. She doesn't bother with difficulties.'

I knew that my mother had to trust me and Fanny to be intelligent enough to look after ourselves, but I realised too that my mother had decided that Aunt Mimi, in her unpredictable way, would keep a strict eye on the two of us. More – she would use her own methods to deal with me and my problem because Aunt Mimi didn't believe in other peoples' rules and regulations. On arrival she had told us, 'You must always do what you have to do, and never do what you mustn't do, because I don't always say no and I don't always say yes. But if I ever do – that's it.'

We knew her well enough to work that out as a free rein to do what we liked, providing we told her what we were doing and accepted her yes or no and obeyed whatever plans she had to help me move myself. There had been no embrace on our arrival, no apparent interest in my condition, not even curiosity at our growth since we last saw her. Nonetheless, I knew there was concern in her usual piercing, almost mocking inspection of us, and she told us to go to our rooms upstairs. 'And watch out for Clothilde,' she added. 'She is in a bad temper today.'

Clothilde had a noble face and a noble authority, but her best defence was her supposed bad temper which meant that she was always on her guard against insults to herself and to Aunt Mimi. She lived in what to me was the best room of the house – on the top where you could see everything for miles around. She had looked after Aunt Mimi for ten years. They were about the same age, but unlike Aunt Mimi, Clothilde had been born and bred in Saint Jean. Her husband had been a fisherman, and like all her family before her she too had been born and bred in the fishing community. She had become Aunt Mimi's housekeeper when her husband was killed in the war. She spoke French most of the time, but when she was angry she broke into her local Provençal dialect which meant that sometimes she was difficult to understand. Clothilde knew everything about everybody on Cap Ferrat, which is why Aunt Mimi also did. When I told Aunt Mimi about the girl from the sea she said, 'That will be the Lelée. She's a little *coquine* so beware.'

'What does *coquine* mean?' Fanny asked.

'She's a gypsy,' Aunt Mimi said. 'And your mother should have taught you more French.' In fact my mother had neglected Fanny's French in her own preoccupations with my father and me.

'Is she a real gypsy?' Fanny asked.

'No, not that. But that's what she is, despite everything. She's a sea gypsy, so you'd better beware.'

'What was she doing down by the Phare?' I asked. 'Why should she throw my spectacles away, and why did she push the dinghy away like that?'

Aunt Mimi, in her long Chinese gown, seemed far

away for a moment under her pencilled eyebrows and she said, 'Lelée thinks the sea around here belongs to her, and it probably does because she almost lives in it, even in the winter. If she's got something in that cave then you'd better keep away from it because she's inclined to be *méchante*.' I knew that *méchante* meant wicked, but less so than it does in English. In fact it could be affectionate.

'Does she really live in the sea?' Fanny asked hopefully.

'Of course not. She lives with her mother on the old "Spaniards" estate above the Phare in a little house that used to be the gardener's cottage.'

'She's mad,' Fanny insisted.

Aunt Mimi liked that. 'Of course she is mad. They call her a sea urchin, a blue fish, and some say a mischief maker. But I've always thought of the Lelée as a beautiful girl who looks after her mother. She hasn't got a father, so in the summer she goes around the beaches selling the cloth her mother weaves, and Clothilde says she doesn't sell it cheap because it's very beautiful. Look over there,' she said.

Hanging like a drape near one of the vast windows overlooking the bay was a length of linen cloth which was there purely for decoration. It was so fine and beautifully woven and so sea-green that it really looked like the sea itself. I had noticed it before, and so had Fanny who had said, 'Look, Beau. It's stunning . . .'

'I've already seen it,' I said now to Aunt Mimi.

'There's another one on my bed,' she said, 'and that one is like a wave in the ocean.' Being a Bretonne, Aunt Mimi embraced anything to do with the sea and believed it had a cure in its heart for almost anything. But she considered it a treacherous friend as well as an ally.

We were now eating dinner, and dinner with Aunt Mimi was an experience. The big dining room had become the living room, as well as Aunt Mimi's cooking and dictionary office. At one end, the large wall of glass overlooked the bay in such a way that we were literally hanging over the water. It too was stunning. The dining-room table was half as long as the room, and always littered with cuttings, papers, notes, books and photographs, and we also ate on it. Fanny and I sat on one side while Aunt Mimi sat on the other. Clothilde kept guard at the far end of the table.

I knew that Aunt Mimi and Clothilde were compiling a dictionary (not a recipe book) of Provençal cooking, and every meal we ate was part of their practical test and investigation of ingredients. Aunt Mimi's kitchen, beyond Clothilde's end of the table, was almost as large as the dining room, and it was always filled with the give-and-take that went into the cooking – spices, oils, vegetables, sauces, lemons, onions, garlic, as well as pots and pans, and other mysterious things that make a kitchen the heaven of food. A lot of it was spread out with more of Aunt Mimi's notebooks and papers on the thick wooden work table deeply criss-crossed with a thousand cuts. What Fanny and I got every day from this delicious food was the daily experiment of one dish or another, regardless of whether it was right or wrong for children to eat.

Today Aunt Mimi said we would be eating Provençal *bouta-couire*, a simple casserole which, Clothilde said, would be the base for every other soup we would eat.

Even now, as we ate the *bouta*, with Clothilde sitting at the far end of the table, it was across the table that she and Aunt Mimi discussed the contents of the meal, while Fanny and I enjoyed the perfections of it. Clothilde was the cook, but Aunt Mimi considered herself the expert so that more often than not a meal became an argument between them. In the time we had been here we had already eaten the Provençal *tripo à la reboulet* (tripe with lamb and vinegar) and *raampau de chambri* (casserole of shrimps) but their arguments and their consultations of books and notes had involved a lot of coming and going before we eventually ate so sumptuously in the dining room.

Now Aunt Mimi said, 'You can ask Clothilde about the Lelée. She knows the girl better than I do because I haven't seen her for some time.'

Clothilde was always dressed in black and always smelled of garlic, which Fanny said was like being in a restaurant, and which I enjoyed because I loved garlic. Clothilde said to us from her end of the table, 'Do not listen to those who call her a thief, only because she is an *écumeur*. But when she sells her mother's cloth it's the others who try to steal from her because she can't read or write.'

I was less interested in her inability to read or write than I was in Clothilde calling her an *écumeur*. Though I knew what an *écumeur* was I didn't know if she meant an *écumeur de mer*, which was a pirate, or an *écumeur de plage*, which meant a beachcomber, and she said, 'For years she has been picking up all things from the sea and the beaches, and she hoards them away in The Spaniards, so now they call her an *écumeur de plage* which she is. But nobody knows what she's got up there in The Spaniards.'

'Why do you call her *the* Lelée?' I asked Aunt Mimi.

Aunt Mimi said, 'Lelée is her father's family name, or was, and that is now her first name. The Provençals sometimes do that to their daughters. I've forgotten what her own first name is, I think it's an English Eliza, or something like that, but it doesn't matter. She has always been the Lelée or just Lelée to everybody, and of course she'll be back.'

Two days later Fanny and I were on the little walk-way cleaning out the dinghy's insides. It had been neglected for years and needed scraping and re-painting. Even fiddling with the boat had a certain satisfaction for me, the engineer, and I was busy on my hands and knees, peering through my spare glasses, when I saw the girl Lelée emerging from the sea again, but this time I finally saw the sea gypsy and the sea urchin in her natural state. She was bronzed to a perfect gold by the sun and sea and the cloudless air, and I was overwhelmed by her stunning beauty. She even looked as if she had brought the sea with her as she stood over me, dripping with it.

'You are English, aren't you?' she said to me in English, and then to Fanny, 'And you are English too?' When Fanny stood up and said, 'Go away,' she laughed and said in French, 'And thou art the little mother who looks after the M'sieur.'

'What do you want?' I said as boldly as I could, but I was already so fascinated and attracted that I still had a curious feeling that she had brought with her from the sea all the beauty of the sea.

'Do you speak French?' she asked.

'Yes . . .'

'Does *she*?'

'Not enough.'

'You need not speak French to me,' she said. 'I will speak English. I also speak German and Italian, and I have brought you these.'

She undid a belt around her waist. Attached to it was a green vinyl sponge bag. She undid the tightly tied top of it and poured into the dinghy half a dozen pairs of spectacles of various shapes and sizes. 'You will have what you want.'

It was so unexpected that I laughed. 'Where did you get them?' I asked.

'The foreigners come here and lose things on the *plages*, so I find them,' Lelée said.

'But I don't need them,' I told her. 'I've got extra pairs of my own.'

'I can see that, but you will need another extra pair so you will take what you want,' she insisted. 'They are all good.'

'They might not be the right lens . . .' I was looking up at her through my own spectacles which were now tied firmly around my head.

'You will try them,' she said again. 'I couldn't find the ones I threw into the sea. It was too deep. So you try and you take one.'

'Don't touch them,' Fanny cried. 'They're probably poisoned.'

Lelée looked mockingly fierce and said to Fanny, 'Little grandmother.' And then, mocking me too, 'Are you frightened of me?'

I knew I had to show some strength and I said, 'Why should I be frightened of you?'

'Then try the spectacles. Here,' she said and gave me a pair.

I accepted the inevitable and tried them on. 'They're no good,' I said.

She took out another pair. 'Do you know who I am?' she asked me.

'You're the *écumeur de plage*,' I told her.

She threw up her hands. 'And what do you say in English for such a thing?' she said, as if anything I told her would be worth an echo.

'You're a beachcomber,' I told her.

'Is that what you are saying to me?' she said.

'You're a smuggler,' Fanny said, 'And you've got something in that cave. Something you stole.'

'If you tell me I steal things I will pick you up and throw you into the sea,' Lelée told Fanny. 'So do not say it.'

'I'm not afraid of you,' Fanny said.

This time Lelée laughed and said, 'Yes, you are, but it doesn't matter.'

'I'm *not* afraid,' Fanny insisted vigorously. 'So what have you got in that cave? Why won't you tell us?'

Lelée shook her wet head like a spaniel shaking water off its back. 'If I told you, then afterwards you will think of telling everyone else. So I will not tell you.'

By now I had gone through most of the spectacles and finally I had found a pair which were more or less the same strength as my own. 'These will do,' I told her. 'But they're gold, and they have a gold chain.' I had put them on and, looking her up and down, I realised that she was wearing a hand-made woven-linen bikini, and she stared back at me as if our mutual inspection was natural and necessary.

'You will have them,' she said and put the others back in her green bag. As she tied it up I asked her why she had snatched off my own spectacles and thrown them into the sea.

'I didn't know who you were, and I thought you were looking for something and would tell the Silvios.'

'Who are the Silvios?' I asked.

She narrowed her wet eyes like a cat and said, 'You don't know anything so I will not tell you. But you have a dinghy and soon I will need to have it.'

'Not this one,' I told her.

She shrugged away my rejection and said, 'I know why you are frightened. I have seen your terrible eyes. They are bad, aren't they, so why are they like that?'

'I was in an accident,' I told her. 'Anyway this isn't my dinghy.'

'I know it isn't. It was the dinghy of M'sieur Escalier, so I will ask Madame for it. M'sieur also had a *pointu* in the Boat House and a big *vedette*.'

'There is no big *vedette* – no motorboat,' I told her. 'Only a *pointu*.'

She looked surprised but she said, 'It doesn't matter. Anyway you can't walk, can you?'

'Of course I can, but not very well.'

'I have seen you trying to walk,' she said, 'and you can only lift one leg and the other with your hands, like a toy.'

'That's because my legs are pieced together with nuts and bolts.'

'Will you get better someday?' she asked me.

I didn't tell her that I was really forcing my legs to walk without a stick. Instead I said, 'Of course I'll get better. I have to.'

'Clothilde has also told me about you,' she said, 'and you were angry, weren't you, when I threw away your spectacles?'

By now I was trying to find a small island of resistance in a sea of despair, so I resisted. 'I don't get angry,' I said. 'I don't want to get angry.'

'But I get angry,' Fanny put in, 'and anyway Beau isn't really frightened, and he's cleverer than you. He knows everything. But you can't read or write, can you?'

'Everybody knows that,' Lelée said, 'so what does it matter to you?'

'Even I can read,' Fanny told her, '. . . a bit anyway.'

'Then you can teach me,' Lelée scoffed and went on,

'Now I will go up to see the Madame Escalier.'

I knew the local Provençal habit of calling people by what they did or owned or worked at, like the Welsh. I remembered that Uncle Theophile had made his fortune in ladders. Almost every *escalier* in France – long, short, foldable, metal or wood or both, even domestic or industrial, had been manufactured by M'sieur Theophile Monnier, so Mimi had remained Madame Escalier although Uncle Theophile was no more. I asked Lelée what she wanted to see my aunt for.

'Clothilde came to get me so I have come,' she said. 'But I did frighten you,' she said to Fanny, 'so I will give you this.' From the top of her bikini she took out a thin chain with a silver ring on the end of it. In the ring was a beautiful little jewelled figure of a sea-horse which moved back and forth as Lelée swung the chain. 'See,' she said. 'It comes from the sea, so you take it.'

It was too attractive for Fanny to resist, but when she put out her hand for it Lelée held it back and said, 'You must not call me a thief.'

Fanny had to think about a retraction and she said, 'All right. But you ought to tell us what's in that cave.'

'I won't tell you, but you can have the sea-horse anyway,' Lelée said. She pulled off Fanny's cotton hat and put the chain over her head. 'Sometimes,' she said, and I knew she was provoking Fanny, 'sometimes you say too much. It's not good for a girl. You shouldn't do it. I will go now . . .'

Then she did an extraordinary thing. She pulled the

top part of her bikini over her head and stood topless while she gave it a good wringing with her hands, and because it was made of woven linen the bikini was heavily soaked with water. She put it back on and did the same with the bottom half, not bothering to turn her back on me. At my age it was all a revelation. But once more it seemed natural because I felt again that everything about Lelée seemed to come from the sea, so I hardly had any response except a sort of disbelief. Fanny was the one who was shocked. When Lelée went upstairs, as if the whole place was as much hers as ours, Fanny said angrily, 'You shouldn't have looked.'

But now I was more concerned to find out what Aunt Mimi wanted with Lelée. When Fanny tried to follow her upstairs I said, 'If you go up there Aunt Mimi will send you packing, so stay where you are till Lelée comes back.'

'All right', Fanny said, 'but I'm too hot out here so I'm going inside to sit in the *pointu* until she returns.'

In the Boat House was the *pointu* which Uncle Theophile had used for his fishing. The *pointu* is above all the Midi fisherman's boat and the French dictionary said it was the kind they have been using along the Mediterranean coast for centuries, the kind of boat Napoleon landed from Elba in. But I knew it well by sight. It is pointed at both ends, and it usually has an engine amidships which is powerful enough to allow the *pointu* to carry or trail nets. Rich amateurs like Uncle Theophile – M'sieur Escalier – had beautified these boats and used them for their pleasure.

So we sat in the *pointu* waiting for Lelée to return and we were clearing out old fragments of fishing lines and rusty hooks and bait tins left in the compartments when Lelée appeared.

'You are called Beau, aren't you?' she said to me. 'Do you think you are *beau*?'

'No,' I said. 'It's short for my family name – Beaumont.'

'But you are *beau*,' she said, and then to Fanny, 'Isn't he?'

'Of course. Everybody knows my brother is handsome.'

'And you are the little *fantoche*,' Lelée said. '*Fannee-fantoche*.'

'What does *Fannee-fantoche* mean?' Fanny asked.

'You're a little puppet,' I said.

'If she calls me a little puppet I'll call her a big thief,' Fanny retaliated.

'Then you give me back my sea-horse.' Lelée leaned over to take it back but her mocking growl and a show of white teeth were enough to reassure Fanny and she kept a good grip on it.

'What did Aunt Mimi want you for?' I asked her.

'Your Aunt Mimi wants me to be your day mistress so that you will have to do as I say when I tell you, and all the time too.'

'What do you mean that we have to do-what-you-say-all-the-time?' I said.

Lelée waited a moment before replying, inspecting me again as if she was now very curious about me. 'I am thinking,' she said. 'Aunt Mimi . . .' (she obviously liked the name) '. . . Aunt Mimi has told me, and so has Clothilde told me, and now you will tell me, and then I will tell you what we will do. But you . . .' she said to Fanny who had been trying to interrupt, '. . . you are the problem because you will get in the way.'

'What is she saying?' Fanny demanded angrily. 'What is she up to?'

'I don't know,' I said, 'but I'm going up to ask Aunt Mimi.'

I got out of the *pointu* with some difficulty and as Lelée watched me she said, 'Your Aunt Mimi has paid me ten thousand francs, so you must talk to her and I will come tomorrow morning. You don't have to be frightened of me but you don't want to talk to me, do you?'

Without knowing why, I began to feel that all the problems the accident had left me with were somehow becoming involved with this girl. I knew that the boy I had once been, the instigator and arguer, the dangerously restless theorist of anything and everything, had simply gone, gone away in the aftermath. That's why I kept telling myself that I had become a confused sort of echo of what I had been.

'It's not you I'm afraid of,' I said. 'Since the accident I'm afraid of almost everything, and I want to know what sort of a deal Aunt Mimi has made with you.'

'I will look after you,' she said with a little shrug which suggested – what else?

'If Aunt Mimi is paying you all that money,' Fanny said, 'you ought to tell us what you've got hidden in that cave.'

'Why are you telling me what I am to do? It is I who will tell you what to do, and I will tell you what is in that cave only if you can see it.' She watched me cope with the steps leading up to the house as I took them one by one, holding the railing with one hand and Fanny's shoulder with the other. 'Tomorrow,' she called after us, 'we will go in the dinghy and I will row it for you.'

'No, you won't,' Fanny said as she opened the door to the house. 'Beau can row.'

Lelée's mocking laugh was her usual answer to Fanny. 'You're a real Fanny-*fantoche*,' she said, 'but you must look after him, and he can look after me.'

I knew that Lelée had no intention of being looked after by me or anyone else, but much later I would remember her words.

When we finally got to Aunt Mimi in the kitchen she was surrounded as usual by herbs and spices and god-knows-what, and I asked her if it were true that she had paid Lelée ten thousand francs to look after us.

'Of course I did,' she said. 'It won't buy her a new bicycle but she needs the money.'

'But why did you do it?' I asked. 'We don't need looking after.'

Though she rarely explained herself Aunt Mimi told me to sit down and listen. She was seated at the table and I remembered that though she was a Bretonne she was also a Parisienne and I recalled my mother once saying admiringly of her that she was *en pleine floraison* – full bloomed – and that's what she was in her silk Chinese gown with the large sleeves turned back to the shoulders and her soft arms poised over a mess of *courgettes*, tomatoes, leeks, olives, oils. 'Beau,' she said to me. 'You are not a normal boy at the moment, are you?'

'I know that,' I said.

'Do you realise what a different boy you are now to the Beau who was here last time with your father and mother?'

I wondered if Aunt Mimi was being deliberately hard on me, but I decided that she was in one of her moods because the answer was only too obvious. 'I know what I am, Aunt Mimi,' I said. 'Last time I had proper legs and good eyes and I could cope with things, but now I'm useless.' I didn't want any misery in my reply, I only wanted the facts.

But Aunt Mimi went on. 'You are useless because you have become like Fanny who is eight years old and that's not good. You don't do enough of anything.'

'I know,' I said. 'But what's that got to do with this girl?'

'It's because I've been thinking,' Aunt Mimi said, 'and I've decided you have to go to the sea because it cures everything and Lelée comes from the sea, so she will take you to the sea because you can't do anything alone, can you? You're not to spend your time sitting down there in the Boat House. So I think Lelée will get you to do things that you think you can't do. That's what I told her.'

'Can she make me jump when I can't jump or run when I can't run or see when I can't see?'

'No, not that. You are pitying yourself and that's not

like you. Lelée is a strong spirit and she will know what you have to do. And for Fanny too.'

'I still say she's mad,' Fanny said.

'So are you, darling,' Aunt Mimi said, 'which is very good because what Beau needs is a little madness for his eyes and some help for his legs. So I will leave it to her because Lelée knows about the sea and she'll know what is good for you.'

'Why doesn't she have a father?' Fanny asked.

It was then that I heard from Aunt Mimi most of Lelée's history and the tragedy of her father and the peculiar life of her mother up on the hill. 'But why can't she read or write?' I asked. 'What's wrong with her?'

Aunt Mimi frowned, as if my question was a criticism rather than a question. 'Nobody seems to know why she can't read or write. But Clothilde tells me that she is much too clever for some people because apparently she can remember everything. That's why she can speak other languages. I think she learned them selling to the tourists. She goes to a local school that lets her learn in her own way, although they've never been able to teach her to read or write. But now it's becoming a problem for the teachers. They can't get her going forward because now she is going backwards because she's always in the sea.'

'But what is she hiding in that cave?' Fanny demanded again, uninterested in Lelée's problems. 'She won't tell us.'

'I don't know what it is,' Aunt Mimi said. 'But knowing Lelée she'll tell you only if she wants to.'

'Is she still a smuggler?' I asked.

'If she is, she is. But Clothilde doesn't say so.'

'I hope she is a smuggler,' Fanny said. 'Diamonds and emeralds and all sorts of jewels and gold.'

'Pearls from the sea,' Aunt Mimi continued. 'Emeralds, rubies, sapphires from the island of the Count of Monte Cristo. Do you think that's what she is hiding in her cave?'

'No, it's something else,' I said seriously.

'Then she will tell you what it is when she trusts you, otherwise she will give you up and that wouldn't be good.'

And so it began. Lelée appeared next day at breakfast-time and sat down near me at the kitchen table. She took a croissant and put a huge pat of butter in it as if all life was hers by her own kind of right. Then she said to me, 'Today we will go in the dinghy,' and she went on, 'and you must wear your trunks.'

'I'm not going out in the dinghy to swim in the open sea,' I told her.

'But you *must* go into the sea,' she said. 'It's there for you.'

'I can't use my legs, not in the open sea.'

'You won't need your legs,' Lelée told me.

'You do as she says,' Aunt Mimi said.

'But he'll drown,' Fanny protested.

'Fanny-*fantoche*,' Lelée said as she got up. 'Everything

34

is ready in the dinghy. So today I will row you to the cave. You can sit in the front and M'sieur Beau can sit in the back.' With that mocking 'M'sieur Beau' Lelée had given me the name everybody would use thereafter, and even though it was a mockery I knew that it was also a teasing gesture, but I enjoyed it.

After some effort and after a groan or two, I was in the dinghy, with Fanny in the bow and me in the stern, accepting my fate, but I kept my eye on Lelée who used the oars as if the dinghy was an extension of her body. Once we were clear of the jetty she said to me, 'I will give you flippers and you get over the side and into the water.'

I was wearing bathing trunks but I still had no intention of getting into the open water of the bay. I was afraid of floundering around in a panic, but Lelée said, 'You won't sink. You don't have to be afraid.'

'I know all that,' I said, 'but I don't want my spectacles to get so wet that I can't see. I get confused.'

'That's because you are afraid, so you must keep your head above the water,' Lelée said, and she was already pulling the dinghy into the choppy water of the bay.

It was Fanny who said to me, 'Go on, Beau. I'll watch over you.'

'All right, all right,' I said. I pulled on the flippers and poured my body over the stern into the sea. Though I had simply fallen into the water, and though I managed to keep my head up, I yelled because it was the month of May, too early in summer for the water to be warm. 'It's freezing,' I said.

'Why do you talk?' Lelée said. 'You hold the boat and kick.'

What I had been doing as therapy in a London swimming pool had become depressingly medical, but under the blue Mediterranean sky, with the green sea all around me, the joy of it came back and I felt the delight of the boy I had been with perfect legs and eyes, and the embrace of the sea itself that was suddenly a real liberty for a messed-up body like mine, even though I was hanging on to the stern of the boat and trying to work my useless legs.

When we were near the Phare, where the cave was, Lelée stopped the dinghy dead like a bus driver and she said, 'Now we will look in the cave – if you can see it.'

I was already treading water and peering into the sea, looking for the silver streak, but the water was too choppy. 'I can't see anything at all,' I said.

'I can't see anything either,' Fanny said. 'There's nothing there.'

'Don't be so quick, and I am going to show you,' Lelée said, 'but I will put an evil spit on you if you ever tell anybody else.'

She sculled the dinghy close to the rocks and, climbing over Fanny, she took the rope from the bow and leapt onto the rocky ledge above the cave. Here there was a little patch of flat sand with a stake near it. She attached the dinghy to the stake and told me (still in the water) to get up on the ledge.

'Can you do it?' she said.

'Of course,' I replied and though I didn't really believe

it I managed to pull myself onto the ledge, and because she was watching me I had to do it.

Lelée climbed back into the dinghy and tipped up the canvas bag she had stashed away in the bow. Out of it came four dead fish, a pair of underwater goggles, a mask and flippers, a snorkel, a belt with lead weights and a length of rope attached to it.

'You use the water goggles over your spectacles,' she said as she gave them to me. I was still shivering on the rocks but Lelée would never acknowledge any need to shiver in the sea.

'I can't go under,' I told her, although anything underwater had always been one of my joys.

'You don't have to dive,' Lelée said. 'You lie and watch and you will see. Put the snorkel on.'

'What about me?' Fanny said.

'You can't swim, can you, but you can watch,' Lelée told her and pulled out a large box she had pushed under the rowing seat. 'My papa could never swim and he always looked with this.' The box was made of wood but its bottom was a sheet of glass. 'You see,' she said and put it over the side and tied it to a ring on the gunwales.

'What are you going to do?' I asked her.

'I will go down and then I will show you what you cannot see.'

She held up the end of the rope that was attached to the weight belt and told me to loop it over the stake behind me. Then she put on her mask and flippers, tucked the dead fish into her bikini and, after making sure that I was in the water with flippers and goggles, and that Fanny could hold the box, she picked up the weight belt. Taking two short breaths and blowing them out, then two more, and finally a long deep breath she went over the side holding the weight belt.

I knew that by taking and expelling those short breaths she had been venting her lungs to get rid of the latent carbon dioxide. I also knew it could be dangerous to the lungs. But I watched her using the weight belt to get her down fast, her flippers making a mermaid of her as she used her legs like a tail.

Because it was all made clear with the goggles I was amazed to see how deep she went until finally she dropped the weight belt and disappeared into the silver gash. For a very long moment it seemed as if she had not only disappeared but had been trapped, and I wondered how she could hold her breath so long.

But then she came out of the cave with her arms extended, and even as she turned to come up I was sure that I saw the head of a huge fish taking a little fish from Lelée's hand, but then she came up as she had gone down – straight and fast as Fanny cried out, 'I saw it, I saw it,' and Lelée once again took four short breaths followed by a large gulp of air and went down again.

'Did you see it?' Fanny shouted.

'Yes, but what's she doing now?'

It took Lelée longer to get down without the weight belt but once at the cave mouth she didn't go in and I saw her hold out one of the fish, wriggling it as the big fish came out of the cave and took the little fish from her hand. When she offered it another one it slowly, gently, magnificently followed her up, but only half way. It stopped and Lelée continued on up to take and expel more deep breaths. When she went down this time she enticed the fish to follow her up almost to the surface and what we saw was the most beautiful fish I had ever seen. It was a perfect, glistening gold, over a metre long, even larger in the magnification of the sea. Without any hint of movement it simply glided slowly upwards, following Lelée's wriggling fish. It was not only gold, it actually gleamed in the bright light of the sea. Its languid beauty so impressed Fanny that she shouted out, 'But it's lovely, Beau. Look at it.'

'It's a grouper,' I shouted back.

We watched as Lelée played with the fish until it was almost up to us. Then she let it take the fish leisurely from her hand, and as it turned to go it came up and bumped the glass bottom of Fanny's box with its nose and then glided like a ghost to the bottom and disappeared into the cave.

When Lelée pulled herself into the dinghy and took off her mask and flippers, she sucked in a couple of deep breaths and said to Fanny, 'Well, little *fantoche*, did you see what you couldn't see?'

'But it was beautiful,' Fanny said, 'and it came right up to me.'

'It was a grouper,' I told her again.

'It is a *lou dorado merou*,' Lelée said, 'and it is the only

39

golden *merou* ever, and if the Silvio brothers find it they will just spear it and kill it and sell it to the restaurants of the big hotels for thousands and thousands of francs, just to eat it.'

'Who are the Silvios?' I asked her.

'They are who they are,' Lelée said grimly. 'But they are looking for something else. It is only if they happen to find the *merou* that they will kill it and sell it.'

Having pulled up the weight belt she was already making an urgent task of getting the dinghy clear of the cave and she said, 'We will not let anyone see us here. Soon the Silvios will come past in their big Zodiac rubber boat and spy in the rocks with their torches.'

'Spy for what?' I said. 'What are they looking for?'

'I will not tell you now. I will ask Aunt Mimi if I can tell you, because she might think it dangerous for you.'

'But the *merou* . . .' Fanny said. She wasn't interested in anything else. Though I was also fascinated by this beautiful golden fish, I was more interested now in the Silvios and their 'spying', but I didn't want her to ask Aunt Mimi if Lelée could tell us what the Silvios were looking for because Aunt Mimi might say no if it was something dangerous.

'Can't you stop them catching it?' Fanny persisted.

'You be quiet about it,' Lelée said softly. 'We will all be quiet and nobody will know.'

'I swear I won't say a word to anyone,' Fanny said, finally won over completely to Lelée's authority.

But I knew there was more to this than the beautiful

golden *merou*, and much more to the Silvios than Lelée had told us. I knew instinctively that she was afraid of them, which meant that I should be afraid of them too, whoever they were.

CHAPTER 3

In fact Aunt Mimi would tell us who the Silvio brothers were and what they were looking for, and even more important what Lelée was also looking for; but it was Clothilde who said they were dangerous. That would be two days later, and we spent those two days on the water with Lelée who knew exactly where to catch the kind of fish Aunt Mimi and Clothilde wanted for their fish soup. They were preparing the true ingredients and method of cooking the real *boui-abasso* of Marseilles, the Provençal *bouillabaisse*.

What they needed were some of the small 'rock' fish that lived close – in among the rocks and the seaweed –

lou gouaus, *lou direllos* and the *demoiselles* and *lou saspires*; all of them I knew in English as wrasse. These fish were not eaten but simply put into the stock to give it a rich iodine flavour, thereafter they were simply pulped in the soup and their bones discarded.

In those two days Lelée had deliberately kept me in the water most of the time except when we were fishing with rods, sitting on the rocks, and even without my legs I felt as if I were beginning to function again. She had given Fanny the smallest rod, with a floater made from a big porcupine quill to catch the little *gierellos* and the *demoiselles* which Fanny snatched out of the sea with joyous yelps every time she caught one. Lelée had put her in a special place for the *demoiselles* but then, later, we went to another place called Pointe de la Gavinette where Lelée gave me a small underwater *arbalète*, a harpoon gun, and said, 'You put on your goggles and your flippers and you follow me and you won't have to go under very deep.' She too had an *arbalète* and she went on explaining as she donned her mask and flippers, 'Here there are *larbres* and *rouquiers* and they will swim in the grass and are sometimes very still so you watch me and you will see them. But do not miss.'

I no longer argued with Lelée. I adjusted my spectacles and my goggles, closed my eyes, shivered a bit, and then dived down to the seaweed and the hidden rocks. Though I didn't feel my legs moving freely they obviously did, and I was so pleased, that I missed the first fish I fired at. But in the end, when I had shot three and Lelée had six *rouquiers*, we put them all in the dinghy and Fanny said, 'It's all so cruel.'

Lelée laughed as she put them into her bag. 'In the sea,' she said to Fanny, 'the fish eat each other. Then we come and we eat the fish. So why do you pity the fish when you eat them too?'

'What about the *merou*?' Fanny demanded. 'You wouldn't eat him.'

'There is only one golden *merou*, and it is like the sun. Would you kill and eat the sun?'

So we ate the fish in the *bouillabaisse*; in fact it was that night, the night of the *bouillabaisse*, when Aunt Mimi told us about the Silvios. After an argument between Aunt Mimi and Clothilde about the amount of olive oil in the soup, Aunt Mimi put her notes aside and told us there was no dessert after *bouillabaisse* (we couldn't have eaten it anyway) and said, 'From now on you must be careful with Lelée. She has something she wants to do, and Clothilde is not sure you should help her.'

'Smuggling . . .' Fanny cried.

'Wait, and I will tell you.'

Clothilde was clearing away the remnants of the *bouillabaisse* and she interrupted Aunt Mimi, 'The Silvios are *méchants*,' she said, 'and you must tell these children so.'

'I'm doing that,' Aunt Mimi said impatiently as Clothilde bundled the dishes together and mumbled something with her usual bad temper, but it was Provençal so I didn't understand.

'Clothilde thinks it will be dangerous if the Silvios are

watching Lelée,' Aunt Mimi said. 'And she says they are wicked.'

'But who are they?' I said.

'I am telling you,' Aunt Mimi replied. 'But first I must tell you about the night when Lelée's father's boat was smashed by the Customs and he was drowned because he had been looking for something where they smuggle these things in the water.'

'In caves,' Fanny said.

'Caves, and lots of other places between the Cap and Menton which are the contrabandists' secret places. But it seems . . .' Aunt Mimi looked at Fanny as if she wasn't sure if Fanny should hear all this, but there was something of a Breton sea dog in Aunt Mimi and she went on anyway. 'It seems that the Moroccan contrabandists, who had brought in the stuff, had abandoned it off one of the points along the coast when they were being chased by the Customs.'

'What was it?' I asked. 'What did the Moroccans drop in the sea?'

Aunt Mimi waved an impatient hand to stop Clothilde interrupting. 'Clothilde says it was a metal box, and Lelée's father was looking for it the next night when he was sunk.'

'But what about the Silvios?' I asked again, tantalised now by these mysterious brothers. 'What have they got to do with it?'

'They are *cochus*,' Aunt Mimi said, 'which is what they call the criminals of Marseilles. Clothilde has known them since they were boys in Saint Jean, and her cousin

Mario has always been with them. Mario is a big, fat, soft thing, and I will tell you about him . . .' Aunt Mimi hesitated a moment and said to me, 'You should know about Mario because he is the one who watches Lelée and tells the Silvios what she is doing.'

'Of course,' I said, but it was the Silvios themselves I wanted to hear about, not Mario.

Aunt Mimi looked doubtful but she went on about Mario. 'Clothilde says that he has been serving the Silvios all his life because they are the only friends he has ever had. Even at school he was a frightened *timide* and everybody bullied him except the Silvios. They laughed at him because they laugh at everything, but they did his fighting for him and they always looked after him.'

Again Aunt Mimi stopped and this time she frowned and said to me, 'You are not interested in what I am saying about Mario, are you?'

'But I am,' I said. In fact I had forgotten that Aunt Mimi always watched you closely and added-you-up when she was talking to you, and it must have been obvious from the look on my face that I was impatient to hear about the Silvios rather than Mario. So I thought I had better admit it and I said, 'I was thinking of Lelée, and I wanted to know more about the Silvios, that's all.'

'But I'm telling you about the Silvios if you will listen properly,' she said, and she went on, 'I am telling you what Clothilde says about them, and she says they were always street boys, wild urchins. They were orphans, and I know that they were brought up by a terrible

46

grandmother . . .' Aunt Mimi raised her hands in disgust '. . . who couldn't make any order for them so that when they grew up they never knew about right and wrong except for themselves. But they always looked after her, and only when she died did they go off to Marseilles and get into bad company and go to prison.'

'Did Lelée always know them?' I asked.

'Of course. They were all smugglers. And she knows them now, because they have come here looking for that box, even in the winter. Lelée thinks the Silvios know what's in it, even though they don't know where the Moroccans abandoned it. But they think she must also know something, and that's why Mario is always watching her with his sheep's eyes.'

'Does Lelée know what's in the box?' I asked Aunt Mimi.

'Lelée believes what she has to believe,' Aunt Mimi replied in her doubtful way. 'She thinks that the Moroccans always smuggled in boxes of money, American dollars, which is why her father wanted it, and why the Silvios want to get it before she does.'

'But doesn't she have any idea where they dropped it?'

'Nobody knows, and she too has been looking for it for two years. Now she wants the dinghy so she can go along the coast where there are places you can only get at from the sea – only by boat.'

'Then we'll go and find it,' Fanny said, bouncing up and down on her chair, 'and Lelée will have lots and lots of money.'

I knew that it must be more complicated than that. I also knew that owning any amount of foreign currency in Britain or France was illegal. In the 1950s, after the war, even small amounts were so tightly controlled that Fanny and I had been allowed by law only a few pounds worth of foreign money to come abroad. I had often read in the papers about big penalties for anyone caught with more than their allowance, and in France the more the money, the harsher the retribution. So a box full of dollars might be the treasure of Monte Cristo, but it would also mean harsh punishment for whoever was caught with it.

'If Lelée finds the box,' I said to Aunt Mimi, 'and if it is money, and she is caught with it, she'll go to prison, won't she?'

'They will make of her a serious criminal,' Aunt Mimi said calmly. 'That's what Clothilde says, so she is afraid for Lelée and you too. But it's Lelée who hasn't told us everything.'

I knew by now that Aunt Mimi was daringly on Lelée's side in this, whereas Clothilde was against it and I said to Aunt Mimi, 'Did Lelée ever say who her father was doing it for? Who was he going to give the box to if he got it?'

Aunt Mimi tightened her lips, and the lipstick on them divided her generous face into soft eyes on top and strong chin below. 'Lelée will not tell us what she knows, but she is sure it wasn't for the Silvios, and that's why she wants to find it before they do.'

Though Clothilde didn't understand what Aunt Mimi was saying in English, she had a curious talent for always knowing what was being said, and she interrupted her this time to say that the Silvios were *escouades* – and though I didn't know then what it meant, later I would learn that it was the Provençal word for a squad, which was another Provençal expression for a gang. So there was obviously something more to be scared of.

Fanny said to Aunt Mimi, 'You're not going to stop Lelée looking for it in the dinghy, are you?'

'If I let her have the dinghy why should I tell her what to do with it?' Aunt Mimi replied. 'But if I can't tell Lelée I can tell you and Beau not to do what you shouldn't do if it is bad, and that's what I am thinking about now.' She gave me one of her Aunt Mimi looks and mocking me a little the way Lelée did, she said, 'What do you think, M'sieur Beau?'

'Will you let her have the dinghy?' I asked.

'But that is what I am asking you.'

'If you do, will you let us go with her, looking for the box?'

'That's what I think about,' Aunt Mimi said.

Clothilde interrupted again to say, 'You tell them that the Silvios were not friends of the Corsairo, or of Lelée, and that last year they spoiled some nets and crab pots while they do what they do in the sea without caring. They are *foutistes* . . .'

'I know all that,' Aunt Mimi said. 'But now I must decide about it and I'm not sure.' While she hesitated she continued a vigorous argument with Clothilde about the amount of olive oil in the *bouillabaisse*, and as if that were also part of her thinking she said to me impatiently, 'Although I say "very well" to you, and I say you can go with Lelée, I will talk to her to make sure she keeps away from the Silvios, and I must count on Lelée for this.'

'What if we find the box?' Fanny was asking.

'I will tell Lelée that if she finds it she will bring it to me.' Aunt Mimi liked that and she said again, 'What do you think, M'sieur Beau? Do you agree?'

Flattered, even in mockery, I said, 'It's all right for me, but what about Fanny?'

'What do you mean "what-about-Fanny"?' was her response.

'What'll you do if something happens when you're in the dinghy?'

'I can swim.'

'No, you can't, not enough anyway.'

But Fanny persisted. 'You tell him, Aunt Mimi,' she said, 'that I can go with them in the dinghy.'

Aunt Mimi was gathering up her garlic-soaked notes and she said, 'If M'sieur Beau says no to it, then it is no. That is, if he thinks it is too much of a risk for you.'

'But that's not fair,' Fanny cried. 'I'm going to ring London and ask Mama if I can go.'

'You can't do that,' I said quickly. Knowing that if our parents were asked they would probably say that neither of us could go, I said, 'All right, you can come with us, but you have to do what I tell you.'

'I'll only do what Lelée tells me,' Fanny said. 'But what about the beautiful gold *merou*?'

'What about it?'

'You know everything, so you ought to do something to save it from the Silvios.'

When Fanny put a responsibility like that on me I knew I had to justify her faith in me so I told her I'd think of something, 'But if you do come in the dinghy you've got to do as I tell you,' I said again.

But Aunt Mimi interrupted. 'No,' she said. 'You must both do as Lelée tells you, and if she tells you, both of you, one day, that you can't go,' she pointed to Fanny, 'then you can't go. That is all.'

'Okay,' Fanny said obligingly, and we left the problem there because we didn't really know what Lelée had in mind. But I knew what Clothilde meant when she said quietly to me when we were alone, 'If Lelée finds that box, the Silvio brothers will do everything they can to get it away from her. It's more than money for them, so do not let Lelée do anything foolish.'

'I'll do what I can,' I said, cautiously, because I doubted if I would ever be able to stop Lelée doing whatever she wanted to do.

But I was flattered that Clothilde wanted me to watch over Lelée. I knew that Clothilde considered the Silvios a real menace, and she was also worried that Lelée was alone in this – except perhaps for me. And by now I felt the same way myself.

CHAPTER 4

The first thing Lelée had in mind was an outboard motor for the dinghy, and how we got it was a surprise because I finally saw the gypsy's achievement – the flotsam and jetsam gathered by this *écumeur*. More important, at the end of it all, Fanny and I were to catch our first sight of the Silvios' presence.

Lelée had asked me in the morning if I knew about 'machines'. When I asked her 'What machines?' she said, '*Moteurs, hors-bords* – outboards.'

I loved all machines, and I was immodest enough to say, 'I know a bit but it depends on what sort it is.'

'Can you walk up the hill?'

'What hill?'

'To The Spaniards where I live. If you come I will show you the little *hors-bord*. It won't work, so we will see if you will fix it and then we can go to see if the Silvios have come.'

'Let's go,' Fanny said.

'It's not for you,' Lelée told her, 'because you don't have to come.'

'Oh, yes I do,' Fanny said. 'Where Beau goes, I go. That is what my mother told me.'

Lelée enjoyed every response from Fanny and she said, 'Some day you will be rewarded with all the things you want in your English heaven, and with another little sea-horse I will find for you.'

Fanny said, 'I don't want another sea-horse. I only want the one I've got.' Her fear of losing the sea-horse had made her fussy about it, and she guarded it at all times like a cat with a mouse.

Lelée had her solidly minded French bike outside the Boat House and she told me that if I weren't able to walk I could ride. 'You will pedal and I will push, and Fanny-*fantoche* will hold you up.' When I said I couldn't pedal with my stupid legs she said, 'You will pedal because it is only moving your legs. You are clever so you must pedal.'

I managed with Lelée's help to get on the bike, in fact I even managed to use my legs as Lelée pushed and Fanny held my shirt. But it was difficult because of the dirt paths and short cuts and steep roads until, at the top, we came to the brick wall surrounding a large low villa – The

Spaniards, a tiled beauty with a well-watered garden to match. By then I was exhausted but I had finally felt something tingling in my feet which was unusual. Lelée said, 'Take off your spectacles and then you will follow me.'

'If I take the things off I won't see anything – not a thing,' I told her.

'You will see enough, and it's better for you,' she said.

Then Fanny whispered to me, 'Take them off. Then she'll laugh.'

I took off the spectacles and peered into the gloom. Lelée did laugh and she said, 'You are now a *beau taupe*.' I accepted that to be 'a handsome mole', and I laughed. In fact I was still holding onto the bike and forcing my eyes to see so that I could actually follow her route into what seemed to be a dark forest and then to a small, low house which, in its blur, was like a secret yet to be discovered.

She unlocked a green wooden gate, and now that I was determined to see I realised that the usual blur was less a blur and I saw the door of the gardener's cottage where she and her mother lived. Reaching that door was a victory and, even more, I was surprised by the way the house seemed to grow out of the ground. Then, under a sycamore which towered over us, Lelée came to a long stony shed and when she opened its green door and turned on a light I could just see a long white-washed room with obscured window panes and benches aligned along the walls, loaded with objects from the sea.

It was Lelée's Aladdin's cave, and even in a blur I could

see her collection of fragments: rope, nets, oars, buoys, small anchors, flippers, snorkels, masks, and sandals. In the wooden trays, which must have once been used for seedlings, there were bits and pieces of children's plastic jewellery, gilded little chains, brooches, necklaces, belts and even a small toy motor-boat. More than that I couldn't take in, and I said, 'But where did you get all this stuff?' and Fanny was saying, 'Look at this, Beau . . . look at that . . .'

'Never mind about these things,' Lelée said. 'It's all from the *plages* and the sea. But you've got to see the *hors-bord* motor because I can't make it start and go.'

She had taken me to another bench, and when she switched on a bare light above it I saw an outboard motor clamped to a ledge. It was one of the smallest I had ever seen and Fanny said, 'Don't worry, Beau can fix anything.'

Lelée ignored Fanny. 'It misses itself once, or sometimes twice, and then it stops. Or it just starts and stops because it sticks. So you do it.'

'I need my glasses to see what I am doing,' I said, and when I put them on I saw that the little 'Sea-Horse' was not only clean, it was absolutely intact. I asked her first if she was sure it had enough petrol or kerosene, which only needed a practical dismissal in reply. I pulled the starter cord gently and the motor turned, but it was obviously sticking so I gave it a hearty pull and the motor started with one cough and stopped dead. 'That's what it does,' Lelée said.

The tools were there so I took off the spark plug and I

could see that the piston was low in the cylinder. I pulled the cord a couple of times and asked Lelée if she had some bike oil. Being Lelée it was there with the tools. I squirted some of the oil into the cylinder, worked it once, and then put back the plug. I pulled the cord hard and it started and stopped; but the second time it started, and the little engine snarled into life with a lot of smoke. I let it go on for a while then I switched it off.

'I did not know how to do that,' Lelée said.

'I'm only the mechanic,' I told her.

'But you do know everything, don't you,' she said ironically, drily, 'and when you go back to England you will become a big engineer of anything and everything, not so?'

'With a bit of luck,' I said and laughed.

But she went on, 'If I were an English girl, and if I were in England, I too would become an engineer of anything and everything, like you.' She shrugged. 'But I am *not* in England, am I?'

She said it so seriously that though I heard the usual mockery in it I realised that she meant it, and by now I knew Lelée well enough to believe that, given the chance, she would without any doubt become an engineer of anything and everything. So I pointed out to her that she was half English anyway and said, 'Isn't that enough?'

'I am in France,' she said, 'and in France I will never be anything, will I?'

I hated to hear even a hint of despair from Lelée, and I remembered my mother using a French word, *chagrin*, when she was melancholy or downcast, and I realised how deep Lelée's own chagrin was.

It was Fanny who saved her. 'You're as good as Beau, any day,' she said, 'because you know everything too, don't you?'

'I didn't know how to start that engine,' Lelée said.

'But you did get that motor out of the sea,' I said to her, 'so how did you do that?'

As always, Lelée recovered and she said boldly, 'I raised it myself from the bay in Villefranche where the English yacht had lost it in thirty metres but couldn't find it, so they just went away. I got it with my long rope and a big hook and lifted it up. And now,' she said with her usual determination, 'we take it to the dinghy.'

'How?'

'In my *remorque*, the trailer cart behind my bicycle which I have fixed.'

But first she had to start the motor herself to prove it worked, and as she started and stopped it I looked at some of the other wooden trays that contained more flotsam from the sea. In one I found a chess set, a good-sized travelling set.

'You didn't get that from the sea,' I told her as she stopped the motor.

'Yes, I did, from a German with fingers missing from the war. He taught me to play on the Beaulieu beach and he gave it to me. Can you play it?'

'Of course I can.'

'Then one day we will play and I will beat you.'

I knew she was provoking me but I was fairly good at chess so I didn't take her seriously. Even so, I was cautious with Lelée because I knew how clever-minded she was although in the end we never did play. Then I said something that seemed natural at the time, and looking back on it I realise that I was thoughtless or insensitive, even though in the end it was the best thing I could have done. I had been looking into another tray with tattered books in it, some French but mostly German 'crimmies' or English detective stories, and I said, 'Why can't you read and write?'

She was busy undoing the outboard from the ledge but she stopped and said, 'You're not to ask me that. It is not your business.'

My instinct, even admiration for Lelée, told me not to retreat and I persisted. 'But there must be a reason for it, Lelée.'

'What reason? What are you talking about?'

'I don't know what I'm talking about,' I admitted, 'but if you say you can play chess, and you say you can speak German and Italian, why can't you read and write?'

At this point even Fanny was sensitive enough to say to me, 'That's not fair, Beau. If Lelée knew why she can't read and write she would make herself read and write, wouldn't she?'

'Then she ought to find out why, and she'll know what to do about it.' I suppose it was another one of my theories, and Lelée's response was a painful one. 'Now I will go away and leave you,' she said, 'and you can go home, and I will not see you any more.' She had said it in French and she went on angrily calling me a *blagueur* and a coward.

Realising my stupidity I could only say rather help-lessly, 'You can't leave us for that, Lelée. It doesn't really matter what I said.'

It was enough to stop her because she stood very still, holding a spanner in one hand and in the other a greasy and dirty rag. I knew nothing about dyslexia so my approach was probably the worst kind of interference. But I was determined to be ruthless with Lelée because I knew that, like me, she was trapped in a condition that made her helpless. Even though my problem was physical, and hers was more like a black hole in the mind, I knew it must be a hopeless sort of misery that she couldn't escape or overcome or even understand, so I didn't want her to give in to it.

She was still angry with me, but she picked up one of the books from the tray and said to me, 'You think I am ignorant, but I will show you. I will read to you.'

The book she had chosen was a French children's book called *Le Taxi Très Pressé*. Almost before opening it she half-closed her eyes, peered intensely at the open page, and began to read the French story about a little taxi in a hurry, and she was even turning the pages as she read, word-perfect. But I realised immediately that she was not reading it at all but was simply re-telling the story exactly as someone had read it to her, and she could repeat it word-perfect from memory.

'You're not reading,' I told her, determined to persist. 'You're remembering it.'

'How do you know?' she demanded.

'Because it's obvious,' I said.

It was then that tears appeared defiantly on her cheeks and she said, 'Why do you have to tell me when everybody else knows I can't read? So why don't you tell me that something is missing? Why don't you tell me what is wrong with me because I can't help it, can I? Even Fanny-*fantoche* can read things . . .' She picked up one of the sea-stained paperbacks and said, 'I don't know what it says, do I, even if I know one word – or two and three words. But you know everything, every word, don't you,' she said accusingly to me, 'and you think I am stupid. They tried at school but I know I can't do it so I will not try any more. . . .'

'But I can't read,' Fanny interrupted. 'I just say I can. . . .'

'Do not say that,' Lelée told her angrily. 'You know you can read something, even the words which you know. You are only saying you can't read because I can't read. Some day, someone will laugh at me in my face, and some day I will not be able to write my name, because I can't. And some day when I must be able to read one of the things that I must read, I will die because I am too stupid.'

By now Fanny herself was in quiet tears, and it rescued Lelée. 'Why are you weeping like that?' she said. 'What have I said to you?'

'Because it's just awful for you,' Fanny said. Then, with

Fanny's true faith and her real conviction, she said, 'But Beau can do something, I know he can.'

'You don't say,' Lelée said mockingly, 'What can he do?'

'Beau: you can do something for Lelée, can't you?' Fanny insisted.

'How should I know?' I said angrily, desperately. 'I'll try to think of something, but that's all I can say.'

'But don't you know everything?' Lelée said, and though she was still mocking me I was glad of it because I too was upset to see how deeply hurt she was by my thoughtless insistence. But she was already coming back to life, and when Lelée came back to life it was Lelée emerging from the sea. 'Now,' she said. 'I will go and put the *hors-bord* on the dinghy, and then we will go to see if the Silvios have come back like Marseilles cats.'

I deliberately didn't help Lelée when she wrenched the outboard from the ledge and carried it out to the little box-like trailer attached to her bike. I knew she didn't want any help, so I watched her load the outboard onto the trailer. It was a combination French system that looked French and she told me to get onto the trailer with the outboard, and though I could just manage to get my backside on the edge of the trailer with my legs dangling, she wasn't going to help me and she said, 'Now we will continue,' and she told Fanny to get on the seat behind her and like that we took off. With Lelée pedalling like a rider in the *Tour de France* we plunged down the hill and over the broken paths and short cuts and across the paved roads until, finally, we reached the Boat House.

In fact I shall never forget that thumping, whirling ride because I was aching all over at the end of it. Lelée had pulled the outboard off the trailer and was on the way to the dinghy even as I was still unfolding myself. I went backwards down the steps to the Boat House and this time I fell flat on my face in the dinghy, achieving it with Fanny's help and a few groans, even as Lelée had the outboard on the stern and was ready with the oars to get us free of the walk-way.

'Next time,' Lelée told me, 'you must tell your legs not to be foolish.'

It was an instruction rather than a suggestion, and thereafter I found myself telling my legs not to be foolish whenever they betrayed me. 'Where exactly are we going?' I shouted at her.

'There,' she said, pointing to part of the bay beyond Villefranche.

'If it's the Silvios – what are we looking for?'

'You will see their big Zodiac rubber boat,' she said. 'They will have it, and a *barquette* like this one. If both boats are there they have come.'

'And they will find the *merou*,' Fanny said. 'We mustn't forget the *merou* . . .'

'Why should I forget it?' Lelée said.

'But they might find it.'

'If they do, Fanny-*fantoche*, I will come back and sink all their boats.' But when she told me to start the motor she said to me, 'You didn't think of anything for our golden fish, did you, even though you are clever.'

'Yes, I did,' I told her but I had started the motor and she didn't hear me.

Fanny heard me and she shouted above the noise. 'So what are you thinking?'

'I'll tell you later,' I said as Lelée took us out into the bay and headed for the other side of Villefranche.

It was probably one of the happiest moments of my life, leaning back in the bow of the dinghy, staring up at the million blues of the Midi sky as we chugged across the sun-filled bay of the angels. The sea was a Mediterranean emerald, and all around us the heavy stillness of the summer's hot day was always there, as if everything about us in that beautiful bay would remain as it was forever. And there too, in front of me the creature from the sea, so perfect that I didn't want anything in my life ever to change.

But it changed soon enough. We approached the low cliffs just beyond Villefranche, the side of the bay you couldn't see if you were up on the road. Here the wooded sides came down to a series of small inlets, and along the waterfront were the old Provençal buildings where the locals lived. In each little inlet there were small anchorages of *pointus* and sailing boats. As we turned the point to pass one of these little marinas Lelée suddenly dropped flat on the floor of the dinghy and said to me, 'Come and sit over me, and hold the tiller, but quick. Come quick.'

I was barely agile enough to cover her and I said, 'What's happened?' as she turned over on her stomach to hide her face.

'Keep going,' she said as I took the tiller. 'Don't turn, just go on.'

By now I could see the big, yellow, patched-up rubber Zodiac tied to a small landing, and near it a dinghy like ours. But, more important, and looking at us from the landing, was a big man who was obviously a local.

'Is he one of the Silvios?' I said to Lelée as I felt her wriggling and burying herself under me.

'It is Mario, Clothilde's cousin. He is with them and I don't want him to see me looking for them.' Then she gasped because I was more or less sitting on her, but she went on, 'They must not know I'm spying on them.'

Fanny said, 'I'm not looking, but he's walking away into a shed.'

By now we were almost past the little inlet and Lelée told me to keep going along the coast until we were around the corner. Then she said, 'Cross the bay to the Phare.'

As we crossed the open water, with an American aircraft carrier preparing to up anchor, Lelée was still groaning under the weight of my useless legs, and when we had turned the corner she told me to let her off at the Phare. 'You go back home to your lunch,' she said, 'and I will come later. And don't tell Aunt Mimi or Clothilde anything. I will tell them.'

Instructed, I let her off and headed the dinghy back to the Boat House. Now it all seemed easy, and I was beginning to feel that at last I was doing something active when I tied up the dinghy. Then, having instructed my legs to behave, I was up the stairs quicker than I had ever been.

We found Aunt Mimi half asleep on the big couch with her black cat beside her. Aunt Mimi's cat was like Aunt Mimi, dispassionate, and he ignored everything except his mistress. But as a cat he was an incredible sniffer. He liked to walk around the living-room and the kitchen sniffing in corners like a dog, so he was called the *moucheur* – the sniffer – and Fanny said it was garlic that he was sucking out of the air.

When the *moucheur* meowed Aunt Mimi sat up. She raised one finger from the coverlet of blue mountains (another creation from Lelée's mother) and said of the *moucheur*, 'You must be more careful. He is a *fuyard*, a timid.' Although, like Aunt Mimi, nothing would frighten the *moucheur*. 'So you have been to the bay with Lelée,' she said, 'and you will tell me now what you did.'

I didn't ask her how she knew; I said, 'She wants to tell you herself.'

'Lelée is being a Lou Corsairo, like her father, so you can tell me,' she said to Fanny.

'I can't,' Fanny said. 'I promised.'

'Then Beau must tell me.'

'It's nothing,' I said dismissively. 'She will tell you herself when she comes.'

'Where is she?'

'She's coming.'

'Was she doing something you are afraid of?' Aunt Mimi demanded.

'No, honest . . .'

'Then you can go to the kitchen and get into trouble

with Clothilde for being so late for lunch and I will talk to Lelée.'

I made it to the kitchen where Clothilde was busy cutting and grumbling and talking angrily to herself in Provençal. She ignored us and I guessed she was waiting for Lelée to arrive. I didn't mind waiting because I loved the kitchen. To me it was a laboratory, like my father's, the kind I would have some day, but this one was always spicy and full of the machinery of cooking: pots, pans, jars, scales, cutters, beaters, stirrers, and around the walls Aunt Mimi's encyclopaedic notes, hung on brass hooks; but always there, in permanence, were the delicious smells. At one end, on another table, were the cuttings and photographs and the books of the profession. It was all paradise for an engineer like me.

Fanny whispered that she was hungry and surreptitiously plucked a piece of celery from the cutting board while we waited for Clothilde to give us our lunch. As we sat patiently and silently, Fanny whispered to me again, 'Ask her about her cousin Mario, the man we saw near the Zodiac.'

'Lelée will tell us about him,' I said in reply.

'Yes, but Clothilde is better. She thinks they are all wicked, even her cousin, I heard her.'

'Then you ask her,' I said.

'My French isn't good enough for Clothilde and she's too impatient. Go on, Beau . . .'

So I asked Clothilde about Mario, interrupting her hammering attention on a piece of veal. She lifted the mallet and banged it down as she replied. 'Did Lelée speak to him?'

'No,' I said. 'He didn't even see her.'

'They are going to pursue her like a *limieyo* when she looks for that box in the sea, and Mario himself is a *lacoyo*.' They were two more Provençal words I had to look up. *Limieyo* was a bloodhound, and *lacoyo* was a lackey. Then she followed it with something else in Provençal and more grumbling and finally, 'Mario is the first son of my father's brother, and he is with the Silvios like a spy so that he can watch Lelée for them, but he is a big blunderer and he can't help what he is.'

It was then that Lelée appeared, wearing a woven dress that was little more than a cape, blue with a long gold stripe in it. She said that the iceman delivering block ice and coming from the Grand Hotel had given her a lift, and even as she said it Clothilde was giving her a dressing-down in Provençal, accusing her of something I didn't understand although I guessed it was about the Silvios.

'What is she saying?' Fanny asked.

'Nothing,' Lelée said. She wasn't bothered by Clothilde's outburst. 'She is always angry. She says that Mario knows I haven't found the box so they will be after me again.' Lelée dismissed it with a gesture and went on, 'She wants me to stop searching for the box. She wants me to let it stay in the sea.'

'You can't do that,' Fanny said, 'Don't listen to her.'

Lelée laughed, 'But I do listen to her,' she said. 'Clothilde and Mario are cousins and they were children together. He was always a *pitiable thing* for her, but they would beat each other, and Clothilde says I must not take you in the dinghy to look for the box if Mario is there.'

'That's not fair,' Fanny objected.

'It is fair,' Lelée said, 'but it doesn't matter, Fanny-*fantoche*, because tomorrow I will take you with me to Villefranche *plage* to sell my mother's weavings and you will sell them for me, which will be good for your English-French.'

'That's not the same as looking for the box,' Fanny protested.

I told Fanny to stop fussing. I guessed there was more reason for Lelée's diversion than was obvious because I knew by now that there was often something cunning in Lelée that seemed to be a natural part of her contra-bandist upbringing.

'It will be good if Mario sees me with the dinghy in Villefranche *plage* selling my things. He will think I am using it to sell my mother's weavings. He will guess the dinghy is from the Escalier Boat House and he will know that you are from there, so I will be very innocent.'

'That's all very well,' Fanny said, and she came back to the *merou*, reminding me that I had promised to tell her what I had decided to do about it.

So I told her as we ate Clothilde's *soupo de baneto eme de patavo*, which I knew was a sort of bean soup, 'I read in the *Nice-Matin* the other day that Captain Yves Cousteau is taking over the Oceanographic Museum in Monaco and its famous aquarium, so I thought we could ask him if he and his crew on the *Calypso* could come and net the golden *merou* and take it to the new aquarium. It would be safe there, and looked after, so that everybody can see it and nobody can catch it and eat it.'

'But that's marvellous, Beau,' Fanny said.

Surprisingly, Lelée dismissed it. 'M'sieur Cousteau is a *Capitaine de Vaisseau*,' she said. 'He is always far away in the oceans of the sea, and he is always looking for sharks and dolphins and whales and octopuses, so why should he want a *merou*?'

'If you tell him what it looks like, and what you do with the *merou*,' I said, 'I'll bet he'll want it.'

'If that would be the case then you ask him, not me.'

'But you're the one he'll listen to,' I told her.

I was sure that it would be hard for Cousteau to resist Lelée if she described the beauty of the golden *merou* and told him how she had persuaded it to follow her to the surface.

'You are being adroit again, aren't you,' she said. 'But you didn't know, did you, that Falco, the diver for Captain Cousteau, is sometimes off the Cap in a big trawler boat, the *Espadon*, trying to capture dolphins, so they don't want a *merou*.' She thought about it and said, 'But if you want we will go and ask him, but only if we all go, because you are foreigners and he will listen to you.'

'But when can we do it?' Fanny said. 'Because if we don't do it soon the Silvios might find the *merou* and kill it.'

'We will do it when the time comes,' Lelée said. 'But first we will sell what I must sell for my mother.'

Next morning, after our usual French breakfast (which Lelée made more of with a *baguette* filled with salami and ham and olives), I successfully disciplined my legs and followed the two girls down the stairs to the dinghy which Lelée had already prepared. Lying across one of the middle seats was a hold-all of blue linen which Lelée had obviously brought down from The Spaniards on her trailer.

'You will keep that off the bottom of the boat because it's always damp down there,' she said to me as I made my usual tumbling arrival. 'And put your glasses in Fanny's straw hat because you don't need them in the bright sun.'

I made an elaborate bow to Lelée and obeyed without question, although I did say, 'You're already a sort of blur.'

'But you can see me, can't you,' she said, 'and that's enough.'

It was then, quite suddenly, and thinking of my eyes, that I had a curious feeling that I might have a clue to why Lelée was blind to reading and writing. I had always felt that she actually recognised something in the written page that was there, even single words; the problem was, she couldn't sort out the words except as single, difficult things. Putting them together, making a meaning of them or shaping them into a whole was beyond her. It was like looking at the waves without seeing the sea. With my distorted sight I was in the same situation. I could see small things close up but not the whole. So I decided that what Lelée needed was a pair of mental 'spectacles' so that she could see the sea as well as the waves, the sentence as well as the words. Though it was a crude sort of theory, I wanted to believe that I might find a way to give her the ability to connect the words she could see but couldn't tie together.

But that was yet to come.

As we approached Villefranche, Lelée took the dinghy out into the bay before turning it towards the *plage*, as if to announce to the watchful Mario that she was on her way to sell her mother's weavings. We pulled up on the pebbly, crowded, noisy beach of Villefranche, tied the dinghy to a beach post and carried the blue linen bag up to a little wall where the beach was level. There, Lelée took out a large cloth and spread the rest of the linen on it.

As I put on my spectacles I knew that I would always remember the colour of those pieces, as if grass had grown out of the sea, as if autumn leaves had fallen on the pebbles, or the sun had set softly on the evening sky. But what the pieces were for I didn't know.

It was only when a little crowd of children and bronzed women gathered to look at what was offering that I saw the *commercante* Lelée at work. She shouted at the children to keep away and I soon recognised how ruthless she was with her customers. She distinguished very quickly those who wanted to look but not to buy, those who wanted to buy but couldn't afford the price, and finally those who had the money but intended to pay little or nothing if they could get away with it. But they had no chance with Lelée, and her contempt for these *acheteurs*, these bargainers, soon persuaded them that her prices were fixed. In fact it was the money itself that fascinated me, watching Lelée count thousands of francs in small and large bills.

But it seemed to be a poor day for her. Though some women bought small pieces, and the interested women were keen to handle the cloth and admire it, Lelée said as she began to pack up, 'Today there are no rich Germans, they are all French losers.' But even as she said it, two German women arrived. They told Lelée to open up the bundle again and asked her in poor French what she had. When Lelée replied in German they both laughed and they said something to her in German which provoked Lelée to growl a Germanic reply, even as she undid the bundle and let them see the cloth. They were ecstatic, picking up one piece after another and instantly beginning to bargain, but in the end Lelée treated them as she had the French women – her prices were exact and this time only in German money.

'We didn't bring any German money,' one of them said.

Looking for help one of them turned to Fanny. Having heard her speaking English she said in English, 'You are English, aren't you? So what are you doing with her, and can you explain to her that we haven't any German money?'

'She is my own sister,' Fanny said. 'We are selling her mother's things, so why don't you buy them?'

This time the German woman turned to me and she was amused but friendly, 'Will you tell your beautiful sister that we will come back tomorrow with German money?'

'Why don't you tell her yourself?' I said.

'I did so but she doesn't believe me.'

'I'll tell her,' I said, 'but she probably wants the money now because she might not be here tomorrow.'

'But that would be a pity. They are so beautiful, all the pieces. So then, when will she be here?'

'Ask her,' I said.

'She doesn't seem to like us,' her companion replied.

'Lelée is like that with everybody,' I told her. 'Aren't you?' I said to Lelée.

'I'm not like that, but I will be here after tomorrow, and then you will bring me German money. But for what I said, not what you said.'

I guessed then that they had been trying to bargain in German about how much they were offering in equivalent German marks. When we picked up the bundle to go, one of them said to Lelée in English, 'You are so beautiful, aren't you?' in answer to which Lelée laughed and said, 'Yes I am.'

I thought that would be a good end to the day, but when we were out in the bay and Lelée was singing one of her Provençal songs, almost from nowhere the big yellow Zodiac with its outboards roaring came on us at full speed.

'Look out,' I shouted when it seemed certain to ram us, but it swerved off and swamped us instead with a huge wave. Though the dinghy rocked erratically it was so stable that it didn't go over, but the wave knocked Fanny screaming off her perch in the bow, and Lelée and I were both soaked to the skin. When we recovered we saw the real damage done by that wave.

It had not only swamped the boat, it had soaked the linen bag of the Rabo's linen pieces. It had been thrown off the seat into the wet bottom of the boat and now it was little more than a big sponge. As the Zodiac zoomed off I caught a glimpse of a very large Mario at the tiller, and there were two others in the boat. The one at the bow shouted at us in incomprehensible Provençal as they sped away, and I remembered Aunt Mimi's description of the Silvios as reckless men who laughed at everything they did. It was only a glimpse, but both men were laughing and enjoying our predicament. I wasn't enjoying it, nor was Lelée, but Fanny was excited.

'That was Mario,' she shouted, pointing to the disappearing Zodiac. 'I saw him.'

'That was the Silvios,' Lelée told her. 'And now they have air bottles. Did you see them?'

I had seen the two yellow cylinders of compressed air for diving which were not a common sight. 'I saw them,' I said, 'and now the Silvios will be all over the place.'

'They must be mad,' Fanny said.

'It's that big fool Mario,' Lelée told her, putting the dinghy on course for the Boat House. 'He wants to tip me over.'

'It's the Silvios who want to tip you over,' I said grimly as I tried to do something about the bag of cloth that was soaking wet. 'They were laughing at us.'

Lelée said, 'Leave the cloth,' as she ran the dinghy up

on the beach. Even as I was still fumbling my way out of the boat she was lifting the heavy, soaked bag onto the pebbles. For a moment I thought she would spread everything out to dry, but instead she began to take the pieces out, one by one, and roll them up, squeezing them to get rid of the water.

'You can do this with the small ones,' she told Fanny as she took a square of cloth and made it into a tight little cylinder. 'You must roll them very tight. You do it like this.'

'Why don't I get the hose to rinse them,' Fanny said.

'That's no good,' Lelée said. 'First it must be the sea water because they must be soaked all over, not stained in patches. So you roll the little ones,' she told Fanny, 'and M'sieur Beau will help me with the big pieces and we will try to save them all.'

It required some manipulation to get the large pieces into a neat roll but Lelée didn't spare me and I was as active on my feet and knees as I had ever been. In the end we had all the neat bundles of rolled cloth stacked together. But looking at the wet pile I said to Lelée, 'They're all ruined, aren't they?'

'They are finished as they are,' she said, 'but I will fix them up to sell to the Germans when they are dry.'

Because Lelée was the key provider, or rather the means to providing the money she and her mother lived on, I wondered how much of their livelihood had been lost, and in that curious way she had of showing her response I knew that someone was going to suffer for the damage done. 'If they are making a little war of it for me because they want the box,' she said, 'when the time comes I will make it a little war for them too because I will never let them get the box.'

'We ought to go and sink their big yellow boat,' Fanny was saying.

Lelée laughed. 'M'sieur Beau,' she said, 'will you and I go and sink the big yellow boat?'

'No,' I said. 'You and I will keep out of their way.'

'M'sieur Beau wants to run away,' she said.

I knew she was provoking me but I said, 'You bet I do if that's a sample of what we can expect. They're after you, Lelée, so don't go after them. Just leave them alone.'

'*Toi et Clothilde*,' she said, 'and she isn't even English. If you are afraid, then tomorrow I will give Aunt Mimi back her money, and I will leave you and go back to the sea by myself.'

'You can't do that,' Fanny protested.

'I can do anything, Fanny-*fantoche*,' she said and before Fanny could say anything more she went on, 'When you tell Aunt Mimi yourself what happened she will say that Clothilde is right, and that you would be in danger with me, and that I cannot be your *maîtresse* any more.'

'Then we won't tell Aunt Mimi anything,' Fanny insisted.

'But we must,' Lelée said.

'No, no, no,' Fanny said. 'If we tell Aunt Mimi about it she'll stop everything, even the dinghy, so we don't have to tell her, Beau, do we?'

The two of them were now allied against me, cleverly

putting the final decision on to me, and though I couldn't do anything about Lelée I could worry Fanny. 'What happens,' I said to her, 'if next time we are farther out in the bay, or around the Cap, or on the way to Menton and they tip us right over, what will happen to you?'

'I can swim . . .'

'You can't swim enough,' I told her, 'and I wouldn't be of any use to you.'

'Then Lelée will help me.'

Lelée knew that I was avoiding any decision and she said, 'If you do not tell Aunt Mimi then I will protect you and keep you close to the shore, and I will not go far into the bay or the sea. Is that good enough for M'sieur Beau?'

'Good enough,' I said, 'if that's a promise.'

'If I promise then I do,' Lelée said. She was packing the rolled-up cloth into the linen bag and she went on, 'Tomorrow I will bring a life-saving jacket for Fanny-*fantoche*, and you can wear it all the time, so we can even go as far as Menton in the dinghy.'

'I don't have to wear a life-jacket,' Fanny protested.

'Yes, you do,' Lelée told her. 'If the Silvios come back they may try to sink us.'

'I'm not afraid of the Silvios,' Fanny said.

'But I am, because you can't swim, so if you don't wear a life-jacket you can't come.'

'But they're awful things,' she said to me.

'Lelée is right,' I told her. 'No life-jacket, no dinghy.'

'If it's that dangerous,' she argued, 'then Beau ought to wear one too.'

Lelée liked that. 'M'sieur Beau will keep his flippers on in the boat,' she said, 'so he will swim like a fish, and that will be good enough for him if there is trouble.'

This time I could only laugh. 'All right,' I told Fanny. 'We won't tell Aunt Mimi anything. But you've got to keep well away from the Silvios,' I said to Lelée.

'I know that,' she said, 'but now they are making me angry,' and she put the last damp roll into the linen bag. It was heavy now and I offered to help carry it but she said, 'You go to Clothilde now to get your lunch, and I will come back tomorrow with petrol for the motor and a life-jacket for the *fantoche*, and that's all for today because I must go and help my mother.'

CHAPTER 5

We didn't tell Aunt Mimi anything and next morning with
Fanny in her life-jacket and me with my flippers on, Lelée
took us around the Cap and beyond the Beaulieu beaches
to the bare cliffs and precipitous gaps between Cap Roux
and the Pointe de Cabue where the rocks seemed to grow
out of the sea. There was no way of reaching this spot
except from the sea, and here Lelée suddenly did something she had obviously planned to do.

'La Peenacler,' she said and steered the dinghy towards
a curious pinnacle of rock that stood out among the
others. She tied the dinghy to the base of it and clambered
onto its edge. 'You will watch me,' she said, and using

hands and feet, climbed like a monkey up the side of the thirty feet of jagged rock right to the apex of the Peenacler. Once there she hesitated only a moment, and then stretching out her arms as if to embrace everything around her, she dived elegantly into the dead calm sea.

'What did you do that for?' Fanny shouted at her when she came up near us. We were still in the dinghy.

'Here, I like to make a big hole in the sea,' she said, 'and M'sieur Beau can do it too.'

'Not me,' I told her.

As she pulled herself out of the water I noticed that the top of her bikini had been dislodged by the dive so she simply pulled it off and threw it into the dinghy as she climbed in. 'You are being frightened again,' she said, 'but you must do it.'

'Why?'

'It's good for you. Your mother is French and she would understand.'

'Lelée is right,' Fanny said, prudently concerned to give Lelée back the heart-and-soul of her bikini. 'Why don't you do it, Beau?'

This time I groaned at the strength of their alliance against me but I said, 'All right' and took off my flippers and spectacles and almost fell flat on my face as I got out of the dinghy onto the rock and began a sort of groping climb which I shall never forget. Lelée's bare feet were obviously hardened to the sharp edges of the Peenacler but mine weren't. Half blind, I couldn't even see where to put my feet, and I couldn't bend my legs enough, so that to climb up that jagged pile I had to pull myself up with my bare hands. Halfway up I told Lelée to give me a hand but she said, 'What for? Now it is easy, so you go on.'

I went on, and in the end I reached the top and sat there in a panic and out of breath. When I finally stood up I could just see the obscurity of the water below me, but it might as well have been a London fog. Lelée shouted at me, 'Go on. You must jump.' So I took a deep breath and, after yelling my usual defence against all opposition, I dived into the abyss the way I had always liked to dive – in a jack-knife.

It wasn't perfect, in fact I couldn't quite straighten my legs before I hit the water, but something happened to me when my head went under. Instinctively I opened my eyes, but instead of the usual blur, in a curious flash I saw everything clearly – rocks, sea, even fish. It was like an electric light switching on, but it was real enough even though the usual blur returned when I came up to the surface. In fact I could hardly believe that it had happened, and I decided it must have been an illusion. But in theory, and scientifically, I knew it was something to do with the lens of the sea itself.

'It was marvellous, Beau,' Fanny said. 'We knew you could do it.'

I felt triumphant, but I knew it was really a triumph for Lelée.

She said nothing, and by now we were all on the base of the Peenacler sitting uncomfortably on the spiky gaps. As Lelée put on her mask and flippers she said, 'I will go down now to the bottom to look. You must stay here, Fanny-*fantoche*, and wait, but Beau will follow me with his goggles on.'

She didn't wait for me to get ready but simply disappeared under water, as if the best way to go under was simply to be absorbed by the sea. By the time I got my spectacles, flippers and goggles on she had disappeared, and I only caught up with her when she came up for air and went down again. I don't know how deep it was here but it seemed very deep to me. I watched her winding her way naturally and effortlessly in and out of the crevices in the cliff face, searching for that mysterious metal box, and although it is pointless to call Lelée a beautiful, two-legged fish, that is what she was, coming up occasionally for air so that I was tempted, in sheer admiration, to go down and follow her. But I was too fascinated watching her, and in the end we were so far away from Fanny in the dinghy that I swam back to be sure that she was out of the water and not in it trying to follow us.

'You should have brought me a fishing rod,' she said. 'There are lots of big fish here.'

'We'll bring one for you next time,' I told her.

In fact 'next time' would be the next four days as Lelée took us along the coast searching all the likely places: crevices, caves, weed beds. There were four days to comb the sea before Lelée finally found the box, and with it the sort of problems that Clothilde was afraid of, and which we could only guess at.

But before that happened, each one of those four particular days to come had their own events, beginning that first afternoon at two o'clock when Lelée took us back to the crowded Villefranche *plage* looking for Germans to come and buy the ruined beauty of her mother's art. As we unrolled the cloths Fanny said, 'But they're perfect, Lelée.'

It was true. Every piece looked unspoiled and untouched as Lelée spread them out. Some of them had even taken on a curious, even richer texture, as if sea salt had added something to them. When I pointed it out to Lelée she said critically, 'Now they are rough.' Perhaps they were, but they were still impressive, and when Fanny said enthusiastically, 'Now we can sell them for more and more money,' Lelée laughed and told her, 'And you can sell them for me.'

It became a repetition of the day before. In the fading afternoon shadows trapped under the hills, women appeared from the beach – those who admired but couldn't afford, and those who could afford but wouldn't pay the price. After setting the price for her, Lelée allowed Fanny to sell the small pieces which meant that when Fanny's French (improving every day) became difficult, I became the translator, but in Fanny the women who bargained like experts had met their match.

Then the two bronzed German women arrived, and once again Lelée's German delighted them, and once again I was impressed by its force which I realised wasn't hostile but was simply Lelée's way of thinking in German. 'That's the way they are,' she would say. In fact it became more fluent, if more accented, as the bargaining increased.

The more cheerful of the two, whose name was Charlotta, asked me in English if I understood German. When I said, 'A bit', she said, 'Your sister speaks it like an Alsacienne, but she isn't, is she?'

'She's Provençal,' I said.

The friendly Charlotta told me that her cousin (still bargaining with Lelée) owned a shop in Hamburg and she wanted to buy all the pieces from Lelée, 'But first we want to see where they are made, and your sister refuses to let us, so I thought you might help.'

I hadn't corrected Fanny's claim that Lelée was our sister, but I said, 'They are made by her mother.'

'That's all she will say. But we want to see how it is done because if we want to order more we must know if she can supply it.'

It seemed a fair proposition, but if Lelée had refused it then I was satisfied to do the same and I told the good-natured Charlotta that Lelée's mother didn't like anybody knowing how she weaved the cloth.

'But it's the colours,' Charlotta said.

'It's a sort of secret,' I told her. In fact Lelée had told me that it was the seaweed the Rabo added to the dyes that perfected the colours.

'That's why they are so beautiful. I've never seen anything like them.'

It ended with the two women buying most of Lelée's stock at Lelée's price in German marks, but when they insisted that they must be able to communicate with Lelée I told Lelée I would give them Aunt Mimi's name and address and said, 'That's my aunt, but she knows all about Lelée.'

'That is satisfactory,' Charlotta said, and then she said to Lelée, 'Will you sell me your bikini?'

I wondered if she meant it, and as I watched Lelée's face I almost expected her to say yes and take it off on the spot. Fanny thought so too because she said in a panic, 'She can't do that, Beau. Not here.'

Lelée laughed and said, 'You can buy me, then you will have the bikini.'

Charlotta sighed and said, 'I couldn't afford you. You're too beautiful. But can your mother make me another one?'

'I myself made it,' Lelée told her.

'Then please – you will make another one for me like yours. I am only a little bigger than you are.'

Lelée leaned over and took one of the small green pieces Charlotta and her cousin had bought. 'I will make it from this,' she said, 'but it will cost you more money.'

'This time in *francs-français*,' Charlotta insisted.

'Then you will have to give me a thousand francs and I will make it.'

Like that Lelée settled the end of the day and we got into the dinghy and set out for home, with Lelée teaching Fanny another Provençal song about a sheep that thought it was a swan. But before we reached the Boat House she turned off at the last moment and we went along the coast to the Phare where she tied up the dinghy to the little ledge.

'I will see if the *merou* is there,' she said. 'Then we will know if the Silvios have been diving here looking for the box and have also seen the fish and speared it. But you, our M'sieur Beau, must watch me because I have no weights and no dead fish, so perhaps I will not reach the cave and the *merou* might go out on the other side.'

She was into the sea with mask and flippers before I was ready, but when I went overside I could see Lelée underwater pulling her way down along the cliff face as if she were on dry land rather than in the sea. She reached the cave, but because this side of the bay had lost its sunlight I could hardly see anything at all, and I didn't see the fish. She came up for air, vented her lungs with short breaths, and went down again. This time I went under after her and I managed about ten feet where I could cling to the cliff face, watching for the *merou* as Lelée disappeared into the cave.

My breath was just good enough to hold on, but Lelée was out of the cave in a few seconds and she passed me in a hurry on the way up. By the time I reached the surface Lelée was taking off her mask and breathing deeply.

'You shouldn't vent your lungs,' I told her. 'It's bad for you.'

'I had to go down very fast,' she said.

'Did you see the *merou*?' I asked as we climbed into the dinghy.

'It has gone.'

'Oh no . . .' Fanny cried. 'The Silvios have got it.'

As Lelée started the outboard she said, 'I don't know yet. Sometimes the fish moves further behind the Phare . . . Sometimes.'

'Then let's go and see if it's there before it's too dark,' Fanny said.

'It would be too deep,' Lelée told her, 'and we will not be able to see it.'

'Then we'll come back early tomorrow morning,' Fanny said.

But Lelée shouted above the outboard, 'If the Silvios have taken it I will find out. Clothilde's other cousin will know. He is the *gardien* of the Phare and he's like a sea-hawk so he sees everything from there.'

CHAPTER 6

The next day a Mistral was blowing and Aunt Mimi told us at breakfast that we were not – absolutely not – to go out to sea in the dinghy.

I knew that the Mistral was a gale-force off-shore wind that was not only fierce but took everything out to sea with it. It also blew away the warm top of the sea and allowed the lower and colder depths to surface, so that the sea became icy. But the extraordinary clarity of sky and sea and land made a perfect crystal of the purified air on that early June day.

'But you've been in the sea,' Fanny said to Lelée who was filling a baguette with the usual salami, olives and tomatoes. 'Your hair is wet.'

'I went to the Phare,' Lelée told her. 'Clothilde's cousin says that yesterday the Silvios came in from the sea in their Zodiac but they did not stop.'

'But did you see the *merou*? Did you find it?'

Lelée raised her hands as if to shrug off the question. 'Yesterday other divers were swimming there, hunting for big fish with their guns, and I think they frightened it and it is hiding.'

'That's awful,' Fanny said. 'Maybe they killed it.'

'Don't worry, *fantoche*. If it is a clever fish it knows where to hide.'

'But can you be sure they didn't get it?'

'How can I be sure of that? Fish are also stupid.'

'Then we ought to go and ask Cousteau to come and get it quick.'

'It's no use asking Cousteau to come and get it if it's gone,' I said, pleased with my own idea, but doubtful too because I wasn't sure that Cousteau would help. 'Wait until Lelée finds out if it's still there,' I told her.

'M'sieur Beau is right. No Cousteau,' she said, and once again I wondered about her reluctance to get involved with Cousteau. 'Today,' she went on, 'we will go up the hill to see my mother who wants to talk to you because you are English.'

'Will your mother show us how she makes all those lovely pieces and the colours?'

'My mother will show you everything because you are English like her,' Lelée said. 'She never sees English people.' Lelée seemed to be cautiously protecting her mother when she went on, 'If she asks you for something important you don't have to agree, but you must listen and then she will like you. She is like me.'

I took that as a warning and I didn't look forward to meeting Lelée's mother even if she were English. Clothilde had already told me that the fishermen's wives in Saint Jean had looked after the Rabo. 'But now she is living alone with Lelée, like a ghost in the trees, because she suffers, and she thinks like an English, tranquil, because she is never unbounded like a Frenchwoman, although you can't tell that any more.'

As we set off I wondered why the wives of Saint Jean had looked after her, and why she suffered. But that would come. Now I wasn't sure how I was going to get up the hill. Lelée had suggested we do it as before, with me on the bike pedalling, but I didn't like that and I said, 'This time I'll walk up.'

'You'll be too slow,' Lelée said.

'Then you go on up and I'll see you there,' I told her.

'You'll get lost.'

'I know where the house is,' I told her in my driest voice.

Lelée shrugged. 'In that case it will be good for you,' she said, and Fanny agreed, so they left me feeling resentful that they didn't show more concern, although I recognised self-pity and stopped it.

I knew that my shattered legs, which had been pieced together with metal bolts, were now getting better every day, but I was still stiff and broken. I tired easily as I went up the hill and I had to rest from time to time, and even when I reached The Spaniards I wasn't sure where the two of them were. I didn't want to go into the mother's little house without them so I tried the long shed where Lelée kept her flotsam and her jetsam. The door was open and the two of them were at the far end under a light, bent over some books that Lelée had rescued from the sea. When they saw me Fanny said, 'Look, Beau, Lelée and I are reading one of these old books in English.'

Lelée was quick to correct her. 'I wasn't reading, it was Fanny-*fantoche*.'

'But we were both reading it,' Fanny insisted.

I couldn't believe in either of them reading it so I said, 'What book is it?'

'I told you . . . it's in English,' Fanny replied, 'but we could only read some of the first page.'

I leaned over to look and I was surprised to see that it was a translation of Jules Verne's *Capitaine à Quinze Ans – A Captain at Fifteen*. I already knew the book, I had read it, so I knew the story. 'Do you know what it's about?' I asked them.

'Of course not,' Fanny said. 'That's why we were reading it.'

Glancing at the book I knew that the writing and language of *A Captain at Fifteen* was way beyond Fanny's ability, even more so Lelée's inability. Yet between them they seemed to have been able to do something with the book and I was about to be curious about it when something told me to leave it alone, which I did. But I couldn't quite leave it there because I was too interested in Lelée's difficulties, and I decided to ask Fanny later what exactly they had been doing when she said they were 'reading' the book. And why had she insisted that they were both reading it even though Lelée had denied it.

Then Lelée said, 'Now we will go in to my mother's,' and as she walked ahead I told Fanny quietly to bring the book.

'What for?' she asked.

'Never mind, just bring it,' I told her.

The entrance to what Lelée called her *demeure*, her abode, was a heavy iron gate and, beyond it, the gardener's cottage which was a very low Provençal farmhouse. Even so it had a little tower, a *pigeonier* for keeping edible doves. The door was covered by a panel which was painted with a colourful impression of a fisherman carrying a large fish. The fisherman's outfit and face was a sort of cartoon of a wild *corsaire*, and I liked it so much I asked Lelée who had painted it.

'My mother did some of it for me and I did the rest because it is my father,' she said.

By now I didn't know what to expect when Lelée opened the door but it was rather like entering a small, untidy factory smelling of a concentrated compression of dry yarn – earthy and autumnal. The long room was lined with hand looms and the floor was covered with tins, boxes and drums filled with yarn and spindles, and I soon realised that it was really an ordered sort of chaos. It was also obvious that the long room was three little rooms made into one, and there were more rooms at the far end. But before that, sitting at an oblong table and snipping at a large cloth with tiny scissors, was the Rabo – Lelée's mother.

She looked so like Lelée it was startling, except that the mother was a shadow of the daughter. She was thin to a sort of fragility, but nonetheless, even at a glance, she was alive as Lelée was alive. She wore a black overall dress, but on her head she had a Provençal headdress for widows called a plechium which was like a large, coloured, triangular kerchief that hid her hair. The cloth she was working on was bright orange and green, and she was snipping at its surface with intense, concentrated fingers.

When she saw me she said, as Lelée would have said, 'You are just the right size so later you can help Lelée fold the cloth when I've finished. Lelée is always angry with me because my arms aren't long enough for her. See . . .' She stood up to prove her point and her thin white arms were stained with yellows and reds and greens. Her tight hands were also multi-coloured, obviously from the linen dyes.

'Sit down,' she told me, and already this original of Lelée was instructing me and I liked it. Lelée herself was standing aside like a sentinel, watching and guarding, and the Rabo said to Fanny, 'You are the *fantoche*. And you *are* a *fantoche*, aren't you?' She was amused, and she told Fanny to go with her friend Lelée. 'She will show you the dyes, but put the aprons on,' she said to Lelée. Then, leaning forward to look closely at Fanny, who was already mesmerised, she said, 'You do what Lelée tells you because your Aunt Mimi will come and beat me if you go back to her covered in dye which never comes out.' And then she said to me in French, 'Sit down opposite me so that I can talk to you.'

As she spoke she was watching me the way Lelée did sometimes to see my response, and as I looked back at her I realised that her face and body had been somehow reduced by illness. It had actually tightened everything to make her younger until you looked closer. But I also saw that the headdress she wore was not to cover her hair but to hide it.

As I sat down opposite her she told me that I looked as if I had been too long in the sun, like all Englishmen, and she went on, 'I can't go into the sun any more so I am very pale, but I always like the sun because it gives us everything we have, although sometimes it takes it all back again when it sets.'

She went on talking without interrupting her snipping and brushing, and she asked me if I lived by the sea in England, was my family rich like Aunt Mimi, did I live in a big house, was my Aunt Mimi also my 'imagined' grandmother, and what had happened to my legs and my eyes. 'Are you in pain all the time, even though you look quite *beau*?'

Most of my answers were yes or no, but then she stopped her snipping and looked up at me and said out of the blue, 'When the time comes would you take Lelée to

England with you when you go?' Then, after a moment's hesitation, 'Could you ask your mother if she would have her?'

It was so casually said that I didn't realise at first what she was asking of me. For the moment I could only repeat it to myself: Would I take Lelée to England with me, and would my mother have her? What did she mean? I thought first of Lelée and I said, 'Why do you want her to go to England?'

I suppose my astonishment was obvious, but as we faced each other over the cloth of gold she said in that same off-hand way, 'That's where she could learn to read and write. She would do it there.'

'How would she do it?' I asked.

'I don't know how,' the Rabo replied. 'She is clever at everything, but she can't live here as she is and do what she ought to do. She is not a boy, so she can't become a fisherman like her father because fishermen here are dying out anyway. I don't know what to do with her, because I am like Lelée. I can't help her any more. But your mother will know what to do with her.'

She opened her stained hands and smoothed the gold and green cloth and said, 'I will give this to your mother because it is the English colour for the summer and you can take it with you when you go home.'

It was only then that I began to think of my mother. Why on earth would she want Lelée? She had suffered enough with my father and me, so why should she take on Lelée? It was then that I also remembered Lelée's warning: 'If she asks you for something important you don't have to agree.'

I didn't say anything, and as if she knew that I didn't know what to say, the Rabo simply took off her Provençal headdress and it was almost too much for me because the Rabo had almost no hair except a light gingery crop so that her scalp was almost visible.

'You see,' she said to me as if it explained everything.

I knew nothing about the drastic radiological treatments that robbed people of their hair, I only knew that it was some sort of painful illness that did it. She looked back at me now with a deliberate question in her eyes – one that I couldn't answer. But she had that same mocking smile that Lelée had when probing me, and she went on as if there was nothing more important here than Lelée.

'Do you know that Lelée is not happy here?' she asked me in French.

I shook my head. 'No, I didn't know,' I said.

She went on in English, 'She has no friends because she is too strong for them, even though they all like her. She knows everybody and they know her, and they all understand what she is. They accept her as she is because she is one of them. But she needs to know people who have not known her like that, so that they will *not* say she is all right as she is. She isn't all right, is she – lost to herself because she can't read or write. So every day in England would be a new struggle for her to make herself the way she should be, and you would help her if she went to England.'

By now I was beginning to understand some of the reasons why the Rabo wanted Lelée to go to England, and I said, 'Wouldn't she go mad in England – away from the sea?'

'But it's the sea – the sea is Lelée's trouble,' she said. 'It's the sea that says to her that you don't need anything except the sea. But with its terrible grip on her she will never be able to do what she must do for herself. It is bad for her. Only when she has gone away from it will she learn what she has to learn. In England she could go to a school which is different, or a school for artists because she is clever at that, but I can't help her for that because I am not an artist.'

By now I was ready to defend the Rabo Mireille even against herself so I gestured at the cloth before us and said, 'What is all this then?'

'I am not an artist,' she insisted. 'I am only what they call a *nuanseuse*, a colourist, and then I am what they call a *tresseuse*, a plaiter, because that's all I know.'

'Yes, but you were in an artists' colony,' I said. 'Clothilde told me so, and look what you do.'

'I was never an artist,' she said again. 'I have nothing like that behind me as an old shadow. I came to France when I was eighteen, looking after two children like a faithful dog with the English family who were staying at a villa next to The Spaniards. When they left on a yacht they left me here with Mrs Hetherington who owned The Spaniards and who ran the art colony. She was the one who discovered I knew something about vegetable dyes because I had worked for a year in a dye mixers in Brick Lane in London when I was fifteen. That's where they mixed the old dyes, and when I told Mrs Hetherington about it she said it's what she wanted, and she managed to get some of the vegetable dyes from a *micro-couleur* place in Sète. She got me the copper drums and the *butagaz* and everything I needed to become the mixer for them, like a cheese maker. So I mixed and I also learned to weave. You can see my hands.'

Again she displayed them as if she was proud of them, and though they were little more than bone and skin, her square fingers looked able and strong, and she said, 'You see – they are the hands of a mechanic. You must look at them. So I became a mixer and I would go down to Saint Jean every week to buy the raw yarn for them, and there I met the Corsairo and his mother who sold the yarn in her shop. Then I married the Corsairo and like Lelée he was always in the sea. And like Lelée he too couldn't read or write. That is why Lelée can't read or write. It is the sea, and when he died I didn't want the sea, not any more, and I came up here . . . by then it was all closed up and Mrs Hetherington let me have the little farmhouse, and that was that. Did your Aunt Mimi tell you any of what I am telling you?'

'Some,' I said, 'but not much.'

'Well, she didn't tell you that now Lelée and I must leave here because it will all be sold up, and we will go back to the Corsairo's mother in Saint Jean. She is old now and that will be the worse for Lelée, who will think only of the sea.'

The Rabo held my gaze as if to be sure that I was listening to her, and she said, 'One day Lelée will be lost in the sea if she doesn't go away from it. So she must leave everything in France because here it will always be the sea, and now you can tell your mother everything I have said and she will understand, and you will take Lelée with you.'

I still couldn't take it all in, and if she was saying that the sea was Lelée's shelter from the world, and that it cut her off, then that was about all I could understand. But the Rabo was watching me again with that mocking question, and I wondered why she had told me all this. She must know that I couldn't help her. I wasn't an adult who could decide these things. And even if I could I wasn't sure that I wanted to.

'Why don't you come to England yourself and bring Lelée?' I asked her.

She was standing over me, and as she took off her black overall dress I could see that she was literally holding her frame together, and yet the hint of reckless vigour was still there. 'Now I will show you how I do my plaiting,' she said and, as I followed her to one of the looms, she went on, 'I have nothing to go to in England. I was brought up in a Catholic retreat by the nuns, and I have no parents and no relatives. I ran away from the nuns when I was fifteen, so there is nothing left in England for me now, and nothing of mine for Lelée. But you are now her friends, and if you take her with you she would help your mother. You are also the one she talks about because you are quiet, aren't you, and you watch over her.'

The Rabo had said everything I couldn't say. 'But I can't take Lelée to England,' I said, anxious to make the point, 'and I don't know if my mother could manage.'

We were now facing an oily-looking loom with a half-finished sheet in it and the Rabo said, 'Lelée would make things better for your mother. She is like that. And she would be happy there because she will look after you and the *fantoche*.'

'And what about you?' I said. 'What would you do if she leaves here?'

'I will be with the Corsairo's mother in Saint Jean.'

And that was all she would say. She took my hand and put it on the loom. 'You must put your arm through here and I will show you why a weaver is nothing but a plaiter.'

It began the Rabo's explanation of her weaving, which was more like a mechanic working on a motor than an artist creating something beautiful. It was technical, and yet I knew that it was only half the explanation of what made these extraordinary pieces. It came to an end when Lelée returned with Fanny who was being enthusiastic again, and she said, 'Lelée knows absolutely everything about all the colours, Beau, and now I know how to make all of them, and they're so much better than crayons.'

Fanny had a small stain, a bright red mark, on her left hand, and seeing it the Rabo said to the silent Lelée, 'What did she do?'

Fanny said, 'I dipped my hand in, that's all.'

'Why didn't you have gloves on?' the Rabo demanded.

'I did but it was at the end and I forgot.'

'Then it will be there until you are twenty-two years old,' the Rabo told her. 'Look at my hand . . . See . . .'

But it was Lelée that bothered me now. I think my accident, and nine months of misery, had given me more insight than was normal for my age and I knew, looking at Lelée and her mother, that Lelée would never leave her. But I was thinking, too, that the Rabo was right. The sea for Lelée was simply the sea, and it demanded nothing less of her than Lelée herself.

CHAPTER 7

Everything seemed to take on a new importance after that, even Lelée's search for the metal box. If it was full of money then she obviously wanted it to provide for her mother, now that The Spaniards would be sold and the weaving would stop.

Studying Lelée with a different perception I was beginning to accept her mother's idea that the sea was, in fact, becoming Lelée's enemy, and I was beginning to understand why she wanted to send Lelée away from it. Even so, I wasn't so sure that taking her to a sunless, sealess place like London would overcome her sea-inspired isolation, or her inability to read or write. In any case I was already sure that Lelée would never leave her mother, and *I* certainly wasn't going to do anything that would take her away.

So I decided, in my arrogance or my new understanding, that instead I would do something to make Lelée read. Or rather I would get Fanny to do it – not to teach her but to persuade Lelée to do it as if she were an eight-year-old like Fanny. It was no use doing what teachers had obviously failed to do – trying to teach her as an intelligent girl of thirteen who ought to be able to read. I knew it was another one of my theories, but it seemed to me that what Lelée and Fanny had been trying to do, poring over Jules Verne's book, was really going back to Fanny's age and trying, word-by-word, to put together the story of *A Captain at Fifteen*.

I told Fanny my idea that the best way for Lelée to learn to read was to learn it with an eight-year-old like herself, rather than having an adult trying to teach her as a thirteen-year-old. 'That way it will all come naturally to her,' I told Fanny.

We were eating breakfast. The Mistral was blowing for the second day and Fanny said to me above her croissant, 'That's just another one of your theories.'

'Even if it is,' I replied, 'you know very well that you can't read the book, any more than Lelée can. But if you do it together the way you were doing it, even word by word, she'll learn as you learn.'

'She won't like it,' Fanny said. 'She doesn't want to be an eight-year-old, even if it *is* like me.'

'But you did say that you were both beginning to read the book.'

'We were, but we were only trying to find out, bit by bit, what the words were and what it was about.'

'But did Lelée actually read any of it, word-for-word?'

'Only the words she and I could understand, then she would remember them and try to put them together.'

'But that's the way it would work,' I told her. 'You'd both be on the same level as you begin to read.'

'There she is now,' Fanny said as we heard the door from the Boat House close. 'Are you going to tell her your idea?'

'Better not to tell her anything,' I said. 'Just do it, Fan, when you get the chance.'

'All right,' she said. 'I'll give it a go.'

The chance came later that morning when we went on foot across the pebbles to the Villefranche beach, and because the Mistral blew in force across the bay they had to spread out the cloth pieces one by one and hold them down with stones and pebbles. The beach was almost deserted because of the wind so Lelée didn't have many customers or window shoppers. I was well covered, and reading in French Frederic Mistral's stories about Provence which I had found in Aunt Mimi's bookshelves, and when Fanny produced *A Captain at Fifteen* she and Lelée began to read it while they waited for customers.

I watched the two of them trying to unravel sentences or rather sequences, word-by-word, and with Fanny jabbing her finger on each word, one-by-one, they began to put them together.

Even though it was obvious that Fanny was more advanced than Lelée, that jabbing finger seemed to take them on from word to word although they had difficulty in the first paragraph with words like 'schooner', 'latitude', 'longitude' and 'meridian'. It was Fanny who managed the word 'reputation' but it was Lelée who achieved the word, letter-by-letter, 'harpooner'. In fact Fanny disagreed and said, 'That's not it,' and though Lelée didn't argue Fanny took the word apart and finally agreed, so that when Lelée said, 'What about this one?' to some other word, Fanny replied, 'I don't know, so what does it look like to you?' When they finally put the difficult word in the context of the words before and after, it was Lelée who understood that the combination was 'being able to manoeuvre . . .'

They were still involved in their puzzle of words and sentences, with Fanny lying on the pebbles and Lelée squatting like a frog beside her, when the friendly German, Charlotta, wrapped in a beach jacket, sat down near them and said to Lelée, 'I came for my bikini.' And then, 'But what are you doing?'

'Reading,' Fanny said.

Charlotta looked at the book and said to them, 'But you should be reading that in French if it is by Jules Verne.'

'It's good practice for English,' I said quickly to save any more honest answer from Fanny.

'Then you ought to be reading an English book,' Charlotta told them.

By now Lelée was rummaging in her sack and she said, 'It is here. I will give you your bikini and you will pay me.'

'Let me look at it first,' Charlotta said, and as Lelée handed it to her Charlotta held it up. 'It's lovely,' she cried enthusiastically, but as she inspected it she added, 'The stitching is bad. It's all loose.'

Lelée's contempt this time was professional. 'It is loose,' she said, 'because the thread will shrink when it all gets wet. Then it will be tight. That is why it's like that. But if you don't want it I will take it back.' She took it brusquely from Charlotta's hands.

'Wait,' Charlotta said. 'I'm sure it will be all right but you should have told me. Please . . .' She took it back as Lelée said, 'All right, but now you pay me.'

Charlotta laughed as she handed over the money, 'You are a very good businesswoman,' she said, and though she obviously wanted to continue talking to Lelée she was dismissed when Lelée simply took the money and turned away.

But the bronzed German Charlotta had the last word. As she left she said to Fanny, 'Your sister is a *see-mädchen*, a sea maiden, but that sounds better in German than in English or French.'

Lelée watched her go, and because it was lunch time she said she would have to do something for her mother, so we packed up and went home for a lunch of *soupo de baneto eme de patano* (haricot beans and potatoes), and later, as we were rolling out the dough for *meka à tourto à las Toulousenco* (vol-au-vent Toulouse), I told Aunt Mimi about Lelée's mother.

'But I knew all that,' Aunt Mimi said.

'Why didn't you tell us?' Fanny demanded.

'Because I decided you must see the Rabo-Rabetto for yourselves. I knew her even before she married the Corsairo. She was what Lelée is now, a beautiful girl, and it is sad to see her like a shadow, so I decided that you should see her and talk to her before you hear too much from others.'

'What's wrong with her?' I asked.

'You don't have to know what is wrong with her, but it is something she can't help, because she can't get better.'

'Is she getting worse?'

Aunt Mimi said, 'You shouldn't ask too much, but she isn't getting worse because she will not accept anything worse than she is. She doesn't agree with what is happening to her, so I don't think she will give up fighting for herself.'

'Will her hair grow again?' Fanny asked. She too had been affected, even though she hadn't heard what the Rabo had told me.

'That also,' Aunt Mimi said. 'She once had hair like Lelée's. It was beautiful, golden, English hair.'

At this point Clothilde, who had been listening without understanding the English, said, 'You must tell them how she would hit Lelée with a stick when she was wicked, and that did her good.'

I didn't believe it, but Aunt Mimi screwed up her dark eyes mysteriously and, treating Clothilde's remark as a provocative jest, said to Fanny, 'Does your Bretonne mother ever hit you with a stick?'

'Oh no . . . never.'

'She should,' Aunt Mimi said. 'You are a bold girl, like Lelée.'

'But she did bite me once when I bit Beau, so then I bit him again and he bit me. It was awful.'

Aunt Mimi liked that and translated it for Clothilde who gave Fanny a *morceau* of a vol-au-vent which she had been experimenting with and said, 'Bite this. It is better than a bite from M'sieur Beau.'

It was then that Lelée turned up with two large mullet and she said, 'They were mating. They all chase after each other, lots of them, and they don't care if you are close or not. They become mad with their passion.'

'You shouldn't have been in the cold water in the wind,' Aunt Mimi said. 'I told you not to.'

'The Mistral is dying now, so when I left my mother I was at the Phare.' She turned to Fanny and said, 'The *merou* has come back, and the Silvios are nearby so we will go now in the dinghy to see Captain Cousteau. That is what you want so we will do it.'

Fanny said, 'Let's go.' She had her apron off and was on the way downstairs before I could dust the flour off my face and hands and before Clothilde could pack up some of the vol-au-vent in newspaper for Lelée.

'I'm telling you again to keep out of the water,' was Aunt Mimi's last instruction as I staggered after Lelée. This time I managed to get into the dinghy without falling into it, and we were on our way as Lelée sculled us out into the bay.

'If the Captain Cousteau is not there with the others we will go on to Cap Martin,' Lelée said as she started the motor.

Though the wind had faded into a mere drift, the sea was so flat and blue that it was almost lifeless as we chugged our way around the bay.

As we rounded the Phare, Fanny said, 'Can't we take a look?'

'No,' Lelée said. 'The Silvios are over there near the Saint Hospice and they will see us.'

In fact we met up with the Silvios' yellow Zodiac when we reached the Pointe du Colombier. We were keeping close to the coast leading up to the Pointe de Saint Hospice, but they were closer in and we could see Mario in the stern and the bubbles of the aqualungs breaking the surface.

Lelée guided the dinghy farther out to sea but I said, 'Keep in close, Lelée, never mind about them. Mario has seen us.'

'It's not Mario I think about,' Lelée said. 'It's the air bottles that the Silvios are using now, because they can go deeper and stay under a long time.'

'Just so long as we keep out of their way,' I told her.

'Why should I do that?' she said indignantly.

I knew by now that Lelée intended to defy the Silvios whatever happened, which reminded me of Clothilde's instruction to look after her. But how could I do that when Lelée would always defy anybody who challenged her? What worried me was my guess that the Silvios were as fearless and determined as Lelée. As for myself, out here in the sea I wasn't so fearless because I was aware of Clothilde's other warning – that the Silvios were not only ruthless but they were capable of any wickedness.

But I didn't pursue it when Lelée kept her promise and came back in shore as we rounded the Pointe. Thereafter she kept us among the bathers along the Baie des Fourmis, keeping close to the beaches and near the bare rocks and the wide, steep cliffs. But we kept looking back to see if the Silvios were following us, and it was only when we reached the outer edges of Monaco that we saw the Zodiac with Mario and the two divers approaching. They were coming fast but they went on past us as we swerved into the aquarium's landing where two big boats were tied up. One I recognised as Cousteau's *Calypso*. The other one was the former commercial trawler *Espadon* which Falco, one of Cousteau's oldest collaborators, was using to capture dolphins for the aquarium.

The Zodiac came back, and one of the divers shouted something at us as Lelée tied the dinghy to a big metal ring behind the *Calypso*, which seemed to satisfy the Silvios and they had already gone by the time I got out of the dinghy.

'Take your spectacles off,' Lelée told me, 'and walk up straight like an Englishman. And you, Fanny-*fantoche*,' she said as Fanny got rid of her life-jacket, 'you don't talk. Let Beau do it to Captain Cousteau, and if he isn't there and we talk to his diver Didi Dumont, then I will do it better than you,' she said to me.

Before my accident I had read a story in the *National Geographic* about Didi Dumont coming to terms with a shark in the Red Sea. The shark had circled him and even nudged him, which was often a preliminary to an attack. The second time the shark approached, Didi had offered his glove and the shark took it from his hand. Thereafter it became a one-sided contest as Didi slowly made his way to the surface with the shark following him, but finally hesitating. Then Didi gave it the other glove and tumbled into the waiting dinghy. There were other stories about Didi's adventures with Cousteau underwater, and a photo showed him with his two young daughters who wanted to follow in his underwater footsteps.

Now, as I straightened up and took off my spectacles, my walk became a masterpiece of English poise, although I kept my hand on Fanny's shoulder. But it worked as far as Lelée was concerned, and like that we had reached the *Calypso* just as Cousteau and Didi Dumont were coming down the gangplank.

Seeing all three of us lined up like applicants for his attention, Cousteau stopped in mock surprise and said in French, 'What have we here – *mousquetaires* from the sea?'

Cousteau couldn't have paid us a richer compliment since it identified us with Lelée as things from the sea. Both Fanny and I were, by now, bronzed and sea-soaked like Lelée, but it was Fanny who made the real impression. She was talking before Lelée or I could say a word.

'You have to come and rescue the big golden *merou* Lelée found near the Phare, because the Silvios have air bottles and guns and they will shoot it if they find it and they will sell it to the hotels, and they will eat it. . . .'

'But who are you?' Cousteau asked in English.

'We are staying with our Aunt Mimi,' Fanny said.

'And who is Aunt Mimi?'

Both Lelée and I were bright enough to let Fanny go on and she said, 'She is my aunt. We live on the Cap in the Boat House.'

This time Didi Dumont interrupted her to speak to Lelée in Provençal. I understood enough to hear him ask if she was the Corsairo's daughter, and, as he continued to question her, Cousteau looked at me and said, 'What is the non-stop girl saying about a *merou*?'

I think Cousteau addressed me because I must have looked more impressive than I felt, but I was already over-whelmed by the perfection of the gleaming *Calypso*, and again I was doubtful that this *Capitaine* of his *vaisseau* would bother with our enthusiasm for a fish, however beautiful it was.

But Fanny had no doubts at all. 'It's all true,' she said, 'and Lelée will tell you about it, and about what comes next if the Silvios find it.'

Cousteau was already captivated by the non-stop English *mousquetaire*. He took her arm and said, 'You are the *chef*, so let us go aboard and you can tell me where the *merou* is, and all about what comes next.'

'Wait,' Fanny said. 'Beau can't walk very well. He was in an accident, an explosion, and soon he will be better, but that gangplank is too steep for him.'

It wasn't, but Didi Dumont, a solid man, said in French to Cousteau, 'This other girl is the *jeune contrabandiste* we have always heard about,' and, at that point, he and Cousteau half lifted me under the arms and marched me up the gangplank, Fanny still talking to Cousteau, with Lelée following like a leaf lost in the stream, and I knew already that she didn't like what was happening.

CHAPTER 8

As we sat around the linoleum-covered tables in the
spruce, spicy ward room of the *Calypso*, and as Didi (a
man of few words) told Cousteau (in a few words) who
Lelée was, Cousteau said in English, 'So you are the
Corsairo's daughter, but why are the Silvios chasing
you, and who are they anyway?'

'Clothilde says they are criminals,' Fanny put in.

'They're the Silvio brothers,' Didi told Cousteau.
'They're those two miscreants the English used to call the
Corsican brothers during the war because they got the
English spies in and out of France and were never caught
by the Germans. The Resistance blacked them because

they took money for doing it, but they know every smuggling business along this coast, so if they're here now they must want something badly . . .'

In the Provençal pitch of his voice and in its intention Didi managed to put a curious doubt into everything he said, but he went on to tell Cousteau that what the Silvios were after, and what the Corsairo had been looking for when he drowned, had been lost and nobody had ever found it.

'It's a good *histoire*,' he added sceptically, 'but the Silvios are savages and are unpredictable, so you can't ever tell what *tricherie* they are up to.'

'So that's why the Silvios are chasing you,' Cousteau said to Lelée.

Lelée nodded, but it was a very reluctant nod.

'Are you hunting for the stuff yourself?' he asked her.

This time Lelée said nothing and I detected again the same reluctance in her approach to Cousteau. I had thought at first that she was overawed by Cousteau and his reputation, but knowing Lelée I couldn't believe that she was overawed by anybody. So there must be some other reason. Then it occurred to me that Cousteau – this neat man in white, this *Capitaine de Vaisseau* in the French Navy, and his naval-looking boat which had impressed me, had all the trappings of the authority she had been avoiding all her life.

In fact Cousteau must have recognised something like that because he said quickly to her, 'I'm nothing to do with the bureaucracy, but I'm thinking that if the Silvios are after you I'd be careful because now I remember them.'

'I think they are trying to frighten her,' I said to Cousteau.

'Well, now that I remember who they are they'd frighten me too,' he said, and I realised that Cousteau probably knew every Provençal fisherman and smuggler from Marseilles to Menton because of his activities during and after the war. 'In Marseilles,' he said, 'they call them "The Barracudas".' Then he asked me where the *merou* was.

'There's a cave near the Phare,' I said, and then I told him that it was no ordinary *merou*, because it was perfectly and entirely gold.

'Gold? What do you mean?'

'Just gold,' I said, and I explained how Lelée had dived down deep to the cave and had almost tamed the *merou* to bring it to the surface, 'and when I saw it I could hardly believe it.'

'How deep is the cave?' he asked Lelée.

'It is five or six metres, or some *métrage* like that,' Lelée told him.

Cousteau was surprised. 'If it's six metres, it's too deep for you,' he told her.

'She gets down with a weight belt,' I said, 'and she vents her lungs each time.'

'That's not a good idea,' Cousteau said and went on. 'But if you want us to rescue your golden *merou* how do you think we can do it?'

Lelée looked at me then. 'You tell him what you think, because you know everything.' But before I could reply she went on almost fiercely to Cousteau, 'If the Silvios see you trying to catch the *merou* and you don't catch it, they will come back at night and shoot it for themselves.'

'I can believe that,' Cousteau said. 'But if the *merou* is what you say it is then we ought to save it anyway because all the *merou* along this coast are being wiped out by hunters.'

'But it's beautiful too,' Fanny said, 'so it will be a treasure for you.'

'Why do you all say the *merou* is gold – and you too?' Cousteau said to Fanny.

'Because it *is* gold. All over. I've seen it.'

Cousteau was willing to accept anything Fanny said, but he turned to Lelée then and said seriously, 'It's hard to believe, because I've never heard of a gold *merou*, so we'll have to take a look.'

'You are not to bring big boats down there,' Lelée said. 'They will frighten it away.'

'Don't worry, we won't frighten it,' Cousteau said but he made a gesture of uncertainty to Didi and, half-smiling, said to Lelée, 'If you're worried about the Silvios what is it you are both looking for?'

'It's a box,' Fanny blurted out even as I kicked her under the table.

'If you know it was for the Corsairo, then where is it?'

'I can't tell you anything about it,' Lelée said. 'It's in the sea, that's all I know.'

Cousteau was aware by now of Lelée's hostility, and in his curious, authoritative French way he said, 'If it's a box, what is in it?'

'Lots of money,' Fanny said, despite another solid kick.

'So now you tell me . . .' Cousteau said and this time he laughed. 'And what will the Mademoiselle do with lots of money?'

'She'll keep it,' Fanny said. 'It's for her mother.'

'In fact you are all smugglers, aren't you?' Cousteau said.

'I'm not anything,' Lelée said heatedly. 'But now you will tell the *gendarmes* and the Customs about me, and they will put me in prison.'

Realising that he had gone too far, even with his attitude of half-belief and half-fun, he pretended horror. 'Why should I tell the Customs? If you find the box you can do what you like with it and I will not say anything to anybody. But isn't there some place where you hope to find it?'

'In the sea,' Lelée told him. 'That's all I know, and all I will say.'

By now everything about Lelée was obviously intriguing Cousteau – her beauty, her toughness and her reluctance. Even Didi was involved enough to have taken out a marine chart of the Cap and he said to Cousteau, 'It is deeper than ten metres around there so we will need air.'

Cousteau thought about it for a moment, and the way he looked at all three of us would become my memory of Cousteau whenever I saw him in his films or read his books. It was that little hesitation when he had to decide if he liked or disliked what he saw, and he obviously liked us. 'We can use the *Espadon*'s big, inflatable Zodiac,' he said to Didi. 'But first go on over to the *Espadon* and see what you can find among the big funnel nets they use for the dolphins. Bring the air bottles, and one for the girl, and some *caoutchouc* for her.' *Caoutchouc* was the word they used then for a wet-suit, and he said to me, 'Have you got something in your dinghy to get you into the water?'

'Everything,' I told him.

'What are you going to do?' Lelée demanded.

'We'll see if we can capture your *merou*, but we have to do it today because tomorrow we are leaving for the Canary Islands, so it is now or never at all.'

'Then let's do it,' Fanny said.

'You are the *chef*,' Cousteau said to her as he got up. 'So we'll do it *sur-le-champ* – right away.'

'It's Lelée who is the *chef*, but she'll agree,' Fanny assured him.

In fact for some strange reason Lelée looked at me for confirmation as if I had to share the decision with her. *Trust Cousteau or not*? was in her glance. So I put my glasses on and said, 'It's all right, so let's go.'

We collected our equipment from the dinghy and moved it to their Zodiac which was slapping the sides of the *Espadon*. With not much clumsy help from me it took five or ten minutes to get everything we needed, so that when Didi finally brought out the big open-funnel net

119

Lelée said, 'It is horrible.' But Didi waved a dismissive hand and pointed to the centre of the Zodiac which was virtually a large plastic tank with a hand pump, and he told Fanny in his most disciplined French and with gestures, 'You will pump.' Fanny didn't understand at first but his gestures were enough. His last gesture was to throw four mullet into the tank.

'For your friend,' he said to Lelée.

'They're too big,' Lelée told him.

'Nothing is too big for a *merou*,' he said. 'It would eat itself if it was hungry enough.'

In the Zodiac, Fanny and I were sitting up front and she said to me, 'What if they frighten it away and then the Silvios get it?'

'They know what they're doing,' I told her.

'We shouldn't have done it, Beau,' she said, and, moving closer to me, she made her point by gripping my arm. 'And Lelée doesn't like it, does she?'

It was only too obvious and I said, 'I know, Fan,' and I had to admit to myself that again I was doubtful as we sped like an expedition to trap the golden *merou*.

When we finally reached the Cap at what seemed like a hundred miles an hour in that powerful boat, we turned the Pointe and almost ran into Mario in charge of the Silvios' Zodiac. They were underwater, we could see their bubbles, but as we sped by him Mario was troubled enough to stand up so that he could see where we were going.

'They're here,' Fanny shouted. 'We mustn't let them find it.'

I realised later that when Mario saw us in our Zodiac he decided that we had managed to get some help, and he also thought that we had found the metal box and were on the way to get it. He didn't know that it was Cousteau, and he didn't know about the *merou*, and when Lelée said, 'He will follow us,' she was right. But he didn't come immediately.

When we rounded the Phare and reached the cave Lelée was already in something of a panic, but Cousteau told her to remain calm, and, to reassure her in his professional Naval French, he said, 'But Mademoiselle. You will now know what it is like to be a real fish.'

It was Didi who helped Lelée into the bulky aqualung which hung on her back like a burden after he had persuaded her to put on a *caoutchouc* half-suit which also made her a lump rather than a fish. The weight belt was an additional burden, and when she stood up to go into the water it was Fanny who said to her, 'You look awful.'

It was quite true. Lelée, as we knew her, now looked like a monster. She was no longer a sea creature in the flesh, and the moment Fanny told her what she looked like Lelée was already stripping it all off and she said angrily, 'I don't want it.'

Even Cousteau must have appreciated the difference and, looking normal himself in his aqualung and wet suit and flippers and weight belt, despite his thin body, he said to her, 'All right, no bottles, but don't vent your lungs. You tell us what you usually do and then we'll work it out, but you will decide.'

Didi was already in the water unfolding the big dolphin

net which was longer than himself. Lelée told Cousteau that if the fish was in the cave she would only reach it if she went down with a weight belt. 'But I have to drop it so that I can come up again, so I can't wear it, I can only carry it,' she said, already stripped to her bikini.

Cousteau said, 'Then drop it and we'll pick it up later.'

'The air bubbles from the bottles will frighten the fish,' Lelée said again. 'It might not show itself.'

'I told you, we'll be as careful as sea angels,' he assured her, and as she put on her own mask and flippers I realised that she now seemed as reluctant to capture the *merou* as she was afraid of it being killed by the Silvios, and I was thinking the same thing.

'M'sieur Beau,' she said to me. 'You come in too, but keep Fanny-*fantoche* out of the water. She hasn't got a life-jacket.' And as she got into the water herself she told me it was so cold that it would do me good. 'It will bite you.'

Though I knew all about the cold water of the Mistral it was a shock nonetheless and I was still catching my breath as – with my glasses and goggles – I watched Lelée go down, holding the weight belt in her hand. The sea now was so crystal clear that the cave looked much nearer, and with Didi treading water and holding the net, and with Cousteau holding the other end of it, both filling the sea with air bubbles from the aqualungs, I watched Lelée reach the cave and disappear. Then I waited in that long moment until I saw her emerging with the dead mullet held out for the fish to follow.

It came out in its own dignified way and took the

mullet, and once again I was astonished by its golden beauty as Lelée turned and kicked her way up to the surface. She vented her lungs, despite Cousteau's warning, and went down again, waving her arms at Didi who was too near with his air bubbles. It was when she was enticing the fish up with another mullet that I heard and felt through the sea the vibration of the Silvios' Zodiac approaching us from the Phare.

'It's them,' I heard Fanny cry out.

They were on us almost instantly, and as Mario swerved in behind our Zodiac I got my second good look at him close-up. Even in that glance I could see that he had a childish, almost innocent face, and I think I understood then why the Silvios had enjoyed fighting his battles for him, and why thereafter he had been devoted to them; and also why Clothilde and even Lelée seemed to like him: staring back at us he didn't appear to have any evil in him at all. By now the Silvio brothers were already over the side as if, like Lelée, the sea was their element.

They were forty feet away but I could see Cousteau waving them frantically aside even as the *merou* turned to go down again. But by then Lelée was there with the next mullet, and her presence seemed to reassure it.

'What are they doing now?' Fanny was shouting again as I began to swim towards the Silvios, shooing them off as I approached. I didn't know how I could stop them interfering but by a miraculous effort I managed to kick, or half kick, my flippers in their faces as they hung suspended in the water. They were obviously aware by now that it wasn't the metal box we were after but the fish – a *merou* that we were not shooting at but were trying to capture.

I think the *merou* was confused, in any case it hesitated and stayed where it was, although it retreated when the net came closer. It was then that the two Silvios placed themselves each side of the *merou* as Lelée enticed it with the last mullet and almost gave it a push.

It moved off, but the Silvios almost prodded it back, and because the sea was now alive with the bubbles of four aqualungs the fish obviously didn't know what to do.

I knew it could easily make a dash for it but there was something in the presence of Lelée that I was sure kept it there, and once more when it swerved off to one side it was blocked by the second Silvio. The end came when Lelée enticed it into the gaping hole of the net and Didi closed the end of it.

'What's happening?' Fanny had been continuously crying from our Zodiac, 'Why don't you tell me?'

I took my mouthpiece out and shouted, 'They've got it.'

In fact as the net began to tighten on the *merou* it struggled and Cousteau quickly wrapped the net tighter around its body, even as they brought it to the surface.

Then came another surprise. The Silvios got into our Zodiac and, reaching over the side, they lifted the *merou* into the big wet tank which Fanny had been filling with the hand pump. Cousteau and Didi had been handing the fish up to them, and they had it in the tank by the time Cousteau and Didi were aboard. In that time Fanny had been trying to push them away, shouting at them, 'Go away. Leave it alone. . . .' But I shouted at her, 'It's all right. They were helping us.'

In fact the brothers were enjoying their contest with Fanny, and for the first time I saw their faces as they dropped their masks around their necks. They were both laughing, in fact they were laughing sort of men, and they were obviously twins. I saw them as two cheerful cavaliers with black curly hair and a hard, explosive sort of vigour about them that denied their good nature but explained their contradictions. I knew at a glance that they were tough and ruthless men, and I understood why Lelée was afraid of them.

They began with Cousteau and Didi an exchange of personalities and explorations, half in French and half in Provençal, even as Cousteau and Didi loosened the net around the fish and we could see close-up the real golden beauty of our *merou*. What was rewarding for the three of us was Cousteau's admiration and Didi's reluctant but forceful comment that the *merou* was, in fact, an adornment, but also a default, a freak.

Meanwhile Renato, one of the Silvios, said in French to Lelée, using the familiar thee and thou, 'The Corsairo is dead, Lelée, so the box is not for thee.' To which Lelée replied, also using the familiar, 'Nor for thee, Renato, nor for Guido nor for Mario who put that wave in my boat. But we will get you back like dogs for that.'

The twins enjoyed every word of it, and as if it needed a final response they picked up Fanny and swung her forward and back as if they were going to throw her into the sea, as she shouted, 'Put me down, put me down.' They did so with a bump, and Renato said to Lelée, 'Next time, little Corsairo, we won't swamp you, we will sink you.' It was said as a healthy jest but I knew they meant it.

Cousteau had been too busy with the *merou* to listen, but he accepted the Silvios' humour and he thanked them for their help as they went overboard. They literally dropped into the sea and went straight down as if they suspected that maybe the box was hidden somewhere in the cave where the *merou* had been. And as we took off to return to Monaco, Cousteau made one comment to Lelée saying, 'If you go that deep too often you will ruin your lungs or your ears, and if you vent your lungs like that you will scar them, so don't do it, because you are too young and beautiful to damage yourself.'

'I am better than you think,' Lelée replied, and Didi added his own reprimand, saying, 'Never mind what you think you are. You keep out of the way of those Silvio twins. I think they must know what is in your box, and they will eat you up if you get in their way.'

'But what were they doing?' Fanny kept asking, and when I explained that they had helped us get the *merou* into the net, she said, 'That Mario asked me who was helping us because he didn't know, and when I told him it was the *gendarmes* from Nice he began to hit the water with a paddle to warn the Silvios because he was afraid.'

Cousteau laughed and said, 'I think we will call your big beautiful fish the Fanny-*fantoche*. Isn't that what they call you?'

'That's what Lelée calls me, but you can't do that to the fish. You have to call it after Lelée. It's her fish.'

Lelée said nothing, and it was only later when we had tied up near the *Calypso* that I noticed how despondent she seemed. She said to Cousteau, 'Why must you call it anything? It is a fish. But if you want to call it anything, then you must call it after Fanny-*fantoche*.'

In fact Cousteau was only half listening because he was telling Didi to get some of the crew from the *Espadon* and ask them to get ready the special wet carrier they used for the dolphins, 'And we'll get to the tanks quick.'

It took some time to fill the carrier with water and ease the *merou* into it. Between four of them they carried it into the back of the aquarium and up the stairs to the top of one of the big tanks. We followed them like worried parents with a sick child. The only difficulty was in the net. They couldn't get it off and in the end they had to cut it because the *merou* was obviously disoriented and even stunned. It lay quietly while they removed the net and lowered it gently into the big glass tank.

'It's dead,' Fanny cried as the *merou* lay immobile on its side.

'It will be all right,' Cousteau said and gave it a gentle nudge with his hand.

It didn't move, but then Didi pushed it near one of the hoses pumping air into the water and held it under the bubbles as we all waited to see if our golden fish was going to live or die.

'It's all right,' Fanny cried this time as the *merou*

straightened up and moved its dorsal fins. Then, as if its instinct to go deep had revived, it simply moved down in its effortless way to a corner of rocks on the bottom of the tank, and Fanny said, 'Now it's got a safe place for itself.'

I suppose we all had a right to be pleased with ourselves and we were, except for Lelée. Once again it seemed as if she didn't want any part of the rescue. In fact she even looked miserable, as if she felt that she had betrayed her golden fish, taking it from the open sea to imprison it here in a glass cage. After all, she had gone down to that *merou* summer and winter for more than a year, so her feelings for the fish were the same as the sea-feeling she had for herself.

As we unloaded our goods and chattels from the Zodiac into the dinghy, Cousteau shook our hands and said, 'You can come to the aquarium any time you like, all three of you. I'll tell the bureau to let you in. But . . .' he hesitated, and he went on as if he had changed his mind. 'Never mind . . . you come when you like.'

Finally, Fanny insisted that the *merou* ought to be protected from the other fish in case they didn't like it, and with Cousteau's elaborately courteous agreement to Fanny we left him and Didi and the *merou*, trapped now in the confines of the aquarium. But it occurred to me, as we sped homewards, that we had done to the *merou* what the Rabetto was, in a way, asking me to do to Lelée for her own good: take her away from the sea she lived with, like the *merou* who had lived in it as a wild creature and was now protected and cared for in a big glass cage.

CHAPTER 9

There was one more day to go before Lelée found the box, and we took the time to go back to the two Caps beyond Monaco. Lelée was in the water all morning, with me behind her, and she still dived far too deep with vented lungs which I told her was wrong. But in the end she brought us ashore on a pebbly beach on the side of Cap d'Ail, which was unapproachable except from the sea. There, she and Fanny returned enthusiastically to *A Captain at Fifteen* as they lay on the pebbles.

As I watched them I knew I had been right to suggest it because they were not only enjoying what they were doing, but now it was the story itself they were beginning to follow, and though they must have skipped some of it, only once did they refer to me for help. It was a sentence which needed explaining:

'The main divisions of natural science are botany, zoology, mineralogy and geology . . .' and then, 'In the special confines . . .' When I began to explain what it meant in the story Fanny said quickly, 'Don't tell us what happens. We can find out for ourselves.'

Lelée had still not overcome her dislike for the capture of the *merou*, but she was a good recoverer. On this same day Mario and the Silvios had zoomed by in the Zodiac, taunting us with rude gestures. Fanny, as Lelée's make-believe sister-under-the-skin, said to Lelée, 'They would have found it and killed it if you hadn't saved it, so you must not worry about the *merou* being in the aquarium. Nobody is going to eat it there.'

It was Lelée's laugh that signalled her recovery and we headed home for lunch. In the afternoon Lelée opened out her wares on the Beaulieu beach, and in an hour she had sold enough to satisfy her requirements, much of it to the American women who came down to the sea from the big hotels on the Baie des Fourmis. Sometimes Lelée teased me because there were no wealthy Englishwomen among them, and when a rather modest looking Englishwoman speaking perfect French proved her wealth by buying an expensive little table cover, Lelée said, 'Englishwomen are always black when they should be white.'

'You mean . . . ,' I said, 'Englishwomen seem to be one thing but are really another. Like your mother,' I added.

'Yes, Mama is always like that, and I am like that too, aren't I?'

It was the only time I heard Lelée admit to having anything English in her, and when Fanny said, 'I'm like that,' Lelée told her, 'Of course you are. But you are only half one thing and half the other. That's why you are Fanny-*fantoche.*'

It satisfied Fanny, as anything Lelée said satisfied her, and on the way home Lelée taught her another Provençal song about a tailor from Toulon who sewed himself up in a canvas sack and threw himself into the sea to prove that his stitches were as strong as the sailor's, who was his rival for the maid who looked after the goats. The tailor proved his point by never coming up.

But there was a surprise for us when we reached Aunt Mimi's. On the way up the stairs we heard an echo of Lelée's voice, even before reaching the living-room. It was Lelée's mother, the Rabo, talking to Aunt Mimi who was seated at her long table writing something the Rabo was telling her, and I felt Lelée stiffen. What was *she* doing here?`

The answer came in the same sort of language that Lelée used. 'I came here from the Madeleine Hospital,' the Rabo said, 'and now I am talking to your Aunt Mimi and I am telling her,' she said now to Lelée, 'that you are not to become a fisherman's wife because now I have enough money to send you with M'sieur Beau and Fanny so that you can go to school in England and become more than you are here in the sea.'

Lelée's reply was not resentful nor angry, it was a statement.

'I am not listening to you, Mama,' she said, 'so I do not go to England.'

'But you will,' the Rabo told her and it was odd that though they were arguing, there was no animosity or anger in it as if, in discussion, they were simply different, and the Rabo went on to say, 'Aunt Mimi has said to me *why shouldn't she go to England?* So now we must settle it.'

Aunt Mimi interrupted and told Lelée to go and join Clothilde in the kitchen, 'And you too, Fanny. Beau will stay here with me because he knows about sufferance.'

I knew she meant suffering, but there was no way of disobeying the order; in fact Lelée was obviously glad to disappear, but I wasn't too happy to be left in the middle of something I still didn't agree with and I think the Rabo detected my reluctance.

She was dressed in one of her woven gowns. It looked like a giant leaf, and in it she was less a waif but rather the limb of a delicate birch tree. Her face under its Provençal headdress was a defiant one, like Lelée's, but it also looked over-disciplined in its stark beauty, as if she had just come through some painful experience. Aunt Mimi told me then that the Rabo had been getting her chemical and radio treatment at the Madelaine, 'and she has come here in the ambulance because she wanted to ask me what is the best way . . .'

'No, Madame Mimi,' the Rabo interrupted. 'I want to know the *proper* way.'

'All right, the proper way – the proper way to have Lelée taken in by the Beaumont family.'

The Rabo turned to me then and said, 'I only want to explain what Lelée could do to become a *naturelle* of the family in England, so that it would be good for the Beaumonts and good for Lelée too.'

I wasn't sure what I could say to her, and the best I could manage was to ask, 'Why do you want Lelée to be in our Beaumont family?'

'Because Lelée is like you, M'sieur Beau,' she said in her sardonic way. 'She can be good at everything if she wants to be, and perhaps even your father will know that, when she is there. So you must listen, then you will know her affection for you and your sister, and you will persuade your mother.' She hesitated a moment before saying, 'And Lelée too, because she will listen to you.'

'What does Aunt Mimi say?' I asked, and I said it rather forcefully to both of them.

'Your Aunt Mimi, the Madame Escalier, thinks it is a good idea,' the Rabo said, 'but she can't say yes or no, can she? So what is it that you can say to your mother to persuade her?' she asked me.

I thought about it, deeply attracted as before by this tenacious fragment of a woman, but doubtful of myself. 'I don't know what I can say,' I told her and I was trying to be as honest as I could, 'but I think my mother is tired of problems like me and my father, and though we are getting better I don't think she wants

133

another problem. And anyway, what about Lelée?' I said. 'How will you ever get her away from here? She's like the *merou* in the sea.' I didn't want to mention that Lelée would never leave her mother. In fact, at the time, I was only thinking of Lelée herself.

'Lelée would not be a problem,' the Rabo insisted, 'and she is not a *merou*. She is a girl, and she will help your mother.'

I knew very well that Lelée *would* help my mother because that was what girls were expected to do, but I also knew there would be much more to Lelée than that. 'It won't be the same for her in England,' I said. I didn't know why I was putting up such a fight for Lelée but I was still thinking of the golden *merou*, and I knew somehow that I had to save Lelée from the same fate.

'I know you think it would be difficult for Lelée in England,' the Rabo said, 'but she is used to that. It would be a new provision for her, that's all.'

By now I felt as if I were becoming a part of whatever it was that made the Rabo and Lelée what they were, attachments, but aside from anything else I knew I couldn't simply arrive home one day and tell my mother that I had brought with me a girl from the sea. In the end it was Aunt Mimi who asked the practical questions.

'M'sieur Beau,' she said in her light-hearted way. 'Would you have a room for Lelée in your house in London?'

'No. She would have to share with Fanny.'

'Who makes up your beds?'

'We do, even Fanny.'

'Who cleans the house?'

'Mrs Stone who comes once a week.'

'And what do you do?' she asked me.

'He does everything,' Fanny said, returning from the kitchen. 'He makes things work.'

'It's an old house and I look after it, that's all,' I said.

'So who does all the cooking?'

'My mother and me, and sometimes my father, but he can't cook at all. He's hopeless. Even Fanny gets her own breakfast.'

'So what would Lelée do if she came to live with you like a sister?'

'I don't know,' I said, 'but I suppose, among other things, she would have to help my mother with everything because she is always busy with us. She had to spend all the time looking after my father and me, although it isn't so bad now. In fact my father can get to his laboratory if my mother drives him.'

'If Lelée helped with everything, would it be good for your mother, do you think? Can you tell me?'

'I suppose it would be a help,' I said, trying to be non-committal.

The Rabo had been listening and she said, 'Can your mother get Lelée into an English school?'

'How could she do that?' I said. 'Lelée can't read or write so I don't know what school would take her. I suppose she could always try the French Lycée, because I go there and Fanny will too.'

'But it isn't English.'

I was finally angry and I said to the Rabo, 'Why don't you come to England and do it all yourself?'

Like Lelée, the Rabo was never bothered by anger. She laughed and said, 'I will come to England when my hair grows, but that will be too late for Lelée. I want to ask your mother myself, but she is not here, is she? But you are here, Beau, and if you tell me it isn't good for your mother to have Lelée I will never ask her. Your Aunt Mimi thinks it will be good for your mother, but what is good and bad in England I don't know any more. So I ask you to say what you think.'

I was still angry with the Rabo and I said, 'I was only thinking of Lelée. She will hate England. . . .' But even as I said it I was suddenly deciding, in a curious reversal, that Lelée would be a wonderful companion for my mother, and a devoted sister, which she already was, for Fanny. But I knew that whatever happened she would be Lelée in England as much as she was Lelée in France, and now that she was learning to read it would be a sin (my mother would say) not to continue her education, and that was my thirteen-year-old thinking.

'Lelée will never be just an English girl,' the Rabo was saying as if she knew my thoughts, 'but she'll be an English girl in England and a French girl in France.'

Finally I had to say it and I blurted out to the Rabo, 'But she will never leave you anyway, not the way you are.'

Aunt Mimi, spectacles at full tilt, stopped me. 'Wait,'

she said, and turned to the Rabo. 'What did the doctors at La Madeleine say? Are you any better, Mireille?'

'The one from Le Havre says I am not losing anything of my flesh or my bones or my blood, which is good enough to get on with, but I have to go back in a month.'

When she said that, I looked closely at this diminishing copy of Lelée and I knew she was already living on her hidden strength. 'That's why Lelée will never leave you,' I persisted. 'How can she?'

'Lelée will do what she has to do,' the Rabo replied calmly, and when Aunt Mimi said to her, 'But you yourself can't leave here, can you?' the Rabo shook her head and Aunt Mimi turned to me.

'Tonight I will telephone your mother,' she said, 'and I will tell her she must come here and have her own *vacance*. She needs to come, and so does your father if he wants to, but she has written that he is working so he probably will not come. But your mother will if I tell her and then she can talk to Lelée herself and to the Rabo, yes?'

I knew that whatever Aunt Mimi decided was irrevocably decided, and at this point it seemed to me that all women were very good at irrevocably deciding things, not only Aunt Mimi but the Rabo, Lelée, Clothilde, and even Fanny. So it was fine by me, but I would like to have had help from my father who was also good at deciding things and I said to Aunt Mimi, 'All right, if that's the best way to do it,' and I left her to join Fanny and Lelée and Clothilde in the kitchen.

Between cutting and slicing and stripping and mixing one thing or another, they were also reading *A Captain at Fifteen*, and when Clothilde said to me, 'They'll get that book dirty,' Fanny said, 'A bit of dirt won't hurt it,' to which Lelée responded vigorously, 'But we will not get it dirty.'

I knew that Lelée, at any cost, would keep the book spotless, and it was one of those moments when I wondered how Fanny and I could do without Lelée if she refused to come to England, and if my mother said it was impossible anyway. I didn't want to think about it because, like the Rabo, I too was aware that Lelée was becoming attached to us as if she had now become inseparable from our daily existence. Lelée had become as much my sister as she was Fanny's, even more so perhaps.

CHAPTER 10

The next day was a heavenly June day, the day that Lelée finally found the box, and it began hopefully for me because I got up early, even before Fanny and Clothilde, to have an early morning dip. I was determined to behave as if my legs and eyes were normal, which meant that I refused to stagger, and I didn't wear my spectacles. I knew all about the theory of mind-over-matter, and though sometimes it worked, other times it didn't. This day it did, and I was down the stairs and the steps and into the sea without falling or bumping, and after my swim I got back up again as if, finally, I was beginning to return to normal. In fact I took it as a gift from the sea, from the breathless perfection and beauty of the early morning Midi at its best.

By the time Lelée arrived I was eating breakfast with Clothilde. Lelée had taken her mother home the night before in her *remorque*, but arriving now in the morning she smelled of paraffin.

'That's not a smell for the kitchen,' Clothilde protested. 'You go and wash your hands outside with some *Savon de Marseille*.'

'But that's worse,' Lelée argued. 'They don't mix, so I'll use a piece of lemon.'

'In that case let M'sieur Beau cut it. Don't even touch one of my knives.'

When Fanny arrived it became one more organisation of women, particularly when Fanny said, 'Aunt Mimi just told me that Mama has decided to come down next week. Aunt Mimi says she was talking to Mama this morning, but Papa has to go to work. He's going to Singapore, so he can't come.'

I was glad my mother had decided to come. In a phone call the previous night we had suggested it to her, and her response had been non-committal, but with Fanny begging her to come, and with my pressure, and Aunt Mimi's, it had obviously been enough for her to decide overnight that she would come.

'Is your mother like you, or like Fanny-*fantoche*?' Lelée asked when I had cut her a piece of lemon and she had made her usual sandwich in a baguette with olives, cucumber, salami and tomatoes.

'She's like Fanny,' I replied. 'She never misses anything.'

'Neither does my father,' Fanny said. 'He's like Beau. He's English.' Fanny had said it all in French, and every day now I recognised her increasing fluency as a product of her chattering in French with Clothilde and sometimes with Lelée.

So the day began.

The dinghy was equipped with its usual supply of flippers, masks, goggles and snorkels, and today Lelée had put in a small mask for Fanny, promising Aunt Mimi that Fanny would always wear her life-jacket and that one or the other of us would be watching her. Lelée said, 'She's still too young to be risking herself,' and added a modifier that Fanny, though still a lost petal in the big sea, would soon be a fish with a tail. 'Like me . . .'

'You haven't got a tail,' Fanny said, always exact, but happy nonetheless to accept Lelée's restrictions.

By now I was also a searcher in my own right rather than a follower, and when we reached the last inlet in the coastline of Cap d'Ail I was in the water even before Lelée, promising Fanny that I would be back in five minutes to look after her. Reluctantly she stayed in the dinghy fishing while I searched the turns and twists along the cliffs at about nine feet under, and for the first time I began to feel the strong currents that turned around Cap d'Ail, particularly when I was below seven feet.

I could hear Fanny shouting at me even as I found a large sort of hole in the cliff. I went down to it, almost twelve feet, and here the current was very strong as I groped my way into the big hole. Though my eyes were fairly good underwater, it was too dark to see very far but I could tell that it went much deeper. In fact I was sure there was something in there, and as I came up I saw Lelée nearby and I pointed to the hole and left it to her as I went back finally to get Fanny.

'About time,' she said. She already had her mask and flippers on as well as her life-jacket.

I took her to where Lelée was now diving into the hole, and when we were over the spot we could see Lelée going into the gap, then disappearing the same way she had disappeared into the cave of the *merou*.

'She shouldn't stay down so long,' Fanny said.

'She must have found something,' I replied, although I too was concerned that Lelée was going too deep and staying under too long.

When she finally came up she looked exhausted. She sucked in a big breath and lifted her mask and took two more deep breaths and said, 'It's down there. I've seen it. But it's stuck to the rocks like a big mussel.'

For a moment we were all clinging to the cliff face as the incredulous sank in. 'Can I see it?' Fanny cried.

'It is too deep,' Lelée said, 'and it's in a bad place. There are currents too, so it is stuck there.'

'But can't you pull it out?' Fanny said, swallowing water with every word.

'Not with the dinghy,' Lelée said. 'It will need a bigger thing with a better engine.'

'But you and Beau can do it,' Fanny said.

'And thee too,' Lelée mocked. 'We'll all give it a big pull like sea elephants, and out it will come like a ghost.'

'Don't tease me,' Fanny said.

'Then we'll take you back to the dinghy,' Lelée said, 'and Beau can come and see where it is.'

Protesting, Fanny was taken back to the dinghy where Lelée simply lifted her legs and tipped her in. Then she said to me, 'You will have to take short breaths and a big one like me, and then you will get down deep enough to see it. But you must keep your head straight down.'

I knew it was one of the principles of diving – the head was the heaviest part of the body so you always kept it pointed down. At the cliff face I did as I was told, and I followed Lelée into the hole. After that her flying legs were my guide until I was about to give up. Then I saw the bottom, and there it was.

It was a square aluminium box, very much bigger than I had thought, even allowing for the sea's exaggeration. But it was so jammed into the corner of a crevice that I knew it would take a powerful force to move it. Even as I turned to go up I saw Lelée reach it. There was a lashing of rope around it and Lelée made a hopeless attempt to pull at it, but I was in a hurry to get up because my breath was exhausted.

My first thought when I had recovered my breath and my belief in the impossible was, 'If that's supposed to be full of money there's going to be an awful lot of it.' In fact I couldn't believe it.

I waited and watched while Lelée went down twice

more. Then we went back to the dinghy and sat there recovering, ignoring Fanny's chattering. I knew that Lelée was thinking what I was thinking – how could we get that large box out of that tight hole? And if it was so big and full of money, it was becoming another kind of problem that we needed to understand.

I finally said to Lelée, 'You'll need a crane to get it out.'

'No, we won't,' she replied. 'We'll need the *pointu*. It has a big engine and it will be strong enough to pull it out.'

'All right,' I said after thinking about it, 'but how will we get the box into the *pointu*? It's too big for us to lift.'

'We don't have to lift it. We'll pull it to the Boat House behind the *pointu* like a fishing net full of fish.'

Fanny was finally able to make herself heard and she said to Lelée, 'You'll have to tell Aunt Mimi if you want the *pointu*. Or do you want to sneak it out without telling her?'

'Now you want me to become a thief,' was Lelée's response. But I waited for her real answer, and she made it my problem. 'I will do whatever M'sieur Beau says. If you ask Aunt Mimi,' she said to me, 'she will let us have the *pointu*. So you will ask her.'

I made a mockery of obedience and said, 'Whatever you command. What else can I do?'

Though the *pointu* was bigger and more complicated than the dinghy I didn't ask Lelée if she would be able to manage it. I wasn't going to insult the girl who had lived half her life in a *pointu*. I also knew that Aunt Mimi would have her own ideas about it.

We were still sitting in the dinghy when Fanny said, 'Look, they're over there,' and we saw that the Silvios were diving off the end of the Cap about half a mile away.

'Then we must be very quick to go on looking,' Lelée said. 'Then they won't know we have found it here.' She was already untying the dinghy, and she started the motor to move us farther along the Cap where we spent half an hour diving in full view of the Silvios. We moved a little nearer to them before giving up and speeding home for lunch, but not before one of the laughing cavaliers had shouted something insulting at us which Lelée translated as a Provençal expression saying: 'Better be a fish in the air than a woman in a boat.'

CHAPTER 11

When I told Aunt Mimi over a lunch of *aurado i poumo d'amour* (bream in tomatoes) that we had finally found the box, I tried to make it as casual as I could, making sure that Clothilde was out of the room because I feared her response as much as Lelée did.

'Where have you put it?' Aunt Mimi asked.

'We left it where we found it,' I said.

'Why didn't you bring it? I must see it.'

Lelée couldn't put off the truth any longer and she said, 'It is in a bad place so we will need the *pointu* to pull it out.'

Aunt Mimi didn't hesitate. 'Clothilde,' she called. 'Come in here.'

'But I'm coming,' Clothilde said. She was about to serve the meal. Fanny was carrying the warm plates, and Clothilde the big dish of bream. They put everything on the table and Clothilde said, 'The *fantoche* has told me that you have found the box, which will now give us a lot of trouble.'

'I told her,' Fanny explained, 'because Clothilde will help us.'

Lelée said, 'We don't need Clothilde's help. We only need the *pointu*.'

Thereafter the discussion became what the French call a *salade* as English and French and Provençal arguments became a fierce exchange about the *pointu*, the box, the Silvios, and the real ownership of the box's contents. I was left out of it because I kept out of it until Aunt Mimi put a stop to the arguments and said, 'We will ask the man in the moon what he thinks. So I am asking M'sieur Beau how big is the box?'

I measured it in the air with my arms and said, 'About this size.' I admit it was a deliberate understatement, but I was allowing for the magnification of the sea.

'If it is caught in the rocks, why can't you and Lelée pull it out?'

This time I had to be honest. 'It's too big for that, and it's too deep and it's too jammed in.'

'Then how will you get it out?'

'Lelée will have to attach a rope to it and with the *pointu* we'll pull it out.'

'Can she do it if it's so deep?'

'I will do it,' Lelée said.

'I do not ask you, Lelée, I ask Beau. Can she do it with the *pointu*?'

It was a difficult question to be honest with and I said, 'If she thinks she can then she'll do it.'

'And how in God's favour will you get it here?'

'We will pull it behind the *pointu* like a net full of fish.'

Aunt Mimi still wasn't convinced. 'And the Silvio brothers? What will they do if they see the *pointu*?'

'They'll probably chase us,' I said.

'Then it becomes dangerous.'

'I suppose it might be – if they see us. But they don't have to see us and the box is there, Aunt Mimi. And isn't it what Lelée's father was looking for . . .' I didn't finish the sentence. I didn't remind her that it was the cause of his tragic death, and I didn't say that I understood why Lelée wanted it.

But Aunt Mimi knew what I meant and she said, 'If she wants to get it, and find out what is in it, I will say all right, and she can go and get it. But then we will give it up to the Customs.'

Lelée had been silent and now she said, 'I am only asking you to let us get it up, then afterwards we will decide what is in it and what to do with it.'

I remembered then the practical reason Lelée wanted to find that box – the money in it. It also occurred to Aunt Mimi. 'If you get the box you cannot keep it, Lelée, and if it is so big then how would it be full of money? Perhaps it isn't so. But we must think first of the *pointu* and to find out if it will go.'

148

By the time she had finished saying this, Lelée and Clothilde had begun a bitter argument until Aunt Mimi stopped them and said, 'I know what you are both saying, and Clothilde is right. If you take the *pointu* she must go with you, because you must have a *responsable* with you, so you are not to argue with me. But first it is Beau who will have to make it go. He knows everything about machines.'

I don't know why Aunt Mimi considered me good with machines (probably Fanny) but I wasn't going to deny it. In fact I had been thinking about the *pointu*'s motor and I decided that the real problem would probably be in the shaft and bearings rather than the engine. It hadn't been used for three years so it had not been turned over in that time and it might have seized up. But even if I *were* to be the mechanic I knew that Lelée would have to tell me what to do because she was obviously better with boats than I was and she knew how the *pointu* functioned better than I did. But I suppose in pride I had to consider myself a genuine mechanic after my success with the outboard.

It was Fanny as usual who inspired us when she said, 'Let's go right now and see if it will work.' She was already up and ready to go.

'When you've finished your luncheon,' Aunt Mimi said.

We had been eating the bream and tomatoes with our newly acquired sophistication and appetite, and Fanny said, 'But I've finished everything.' So she had, although the rest of us were still enjoying what was left. In the end it was Lelée who put us in our proper place when she said, 'This afternoon we will not look at the *pointu*. We will sell the cloth at Beaulieu, then we will come tomorrow and fix up the *pointu*.'

'Lelée is right,' Aunt Mimi said. 'Let the Silvios see you behaving as you always do, then they will not suspect anything. You must keep away from them because they'll try to frighten you if they think you are watching them.'

Though I too was impatient to get to work on the *pointu* I knew they were right. So, under orders, we spent that afternoon at Beaulieu selling what was left of the Rabo's cloth, and in the intervals of waiting, Fanny and Lelée went on with their enthusiastic reading which seemed to be getting better fast. It was a short little book but they were almost on page eight when we packed up and went home with the Silvios zooming around us twice, laughing in our faces, so to speak, as they sped home in their yellow, patched-looking Zodiac.

The next morning Fanny and I went straight down to the *pointu* after breakfast and by now I was retreating from all claims that I knew everything about machines because I realised I knew nothing about marine engines. In the last two weeks Fanny and I had spent some time cleaning up the *pointu* and, with my spectacles on my nose, I had taken a good look at the engine. I had managed to remove the engine cover and I was surprised to see how clean and salt-free it looked, and I guessed that Lelée had been at it before me. It was a deluxe *pointu* because Uncle Theophile had spared no expense giving the boat everything including a wheel instead of a tiller. But, of all things, it had an English marine engine called a Morris Navigator. Then I realised that the battery was missing and I wondered if it had a starting handle. In fact I needed Lelée, but she hadn't come for breakfast and she was already so late that I wondered if she had changed her mind about the *pointu*.

'I'll bet she's gone to get something,' was Fanny's explanation, and as usual she was right.

Lelée turned up just as I had found the starting handle, clipped and almost hidden under the cover. I was hand-turning the engine to see if the propeller shaft would rotate. In fact I thought I was doing rather well by the time Lelée arrived, but she didn't think much of my effort.

'You should have put the motor in forward gear not the opposite,' she said. 'But leave it now because you will have to help me with the battery.'

'Where is it?' I said.

'It's in my *remorque*. It is old and it is charged up, but it is too heavy for me to lift down the steps.'

'I'll never believe that,' I said.

'If you joke with me I'll joke with you,' Lelée said, 'and that is not good today, Beau, because we will make mistakes. So you will come and help me, and Fanny can hold the *remorque* while we get it off.'

How we got that heavy battery down to the *pointu* was recorded for me in the argument between Lelée and myself when she shouted at me, 'You're going to drop it,' and my indignant reply when I shouted back, 'You keep swinging it and jamming my fingers.'

'Never mind your fingers,' Lelée said. 'Don't let it tip.'

Lelée had packed the battery in a fisherman's canvas bag, and the problem was to keep it upright because if it had tipped over, the escaping acid would have burned everything it touched, including us, and I told Fanny to keep out of my way as we took it step by step.

'What's the matter? Is it your legs?' she said.

I was staggering onto the last step and I shouted at Fanny, 'Of course it's my legs – they're bruised all over.'

I was glad that Aunt Mimi didn't know what we were doing, and when we had finally lifted it into the *pointu* I knew with a private joy that, despite their punishment, my legs had finally found themselves. My eyes too were seeing most things without much help. The real moment for all our efforts came when we had to start the motor and it was Fanny who said, 'What about the noise?'

'It's not the noise,' Lelée said. 'It will be the smoke.'

She was right. When Lelée pushed the starter button, a large and brutal cough spilled out a cloud of black smoke, then another, and finally after a series of them the engine came to life with a roar that had Fanny holding her ears. We calmed it down, but we were all coughing grimly as Lelée used the engine and gear lever to back us out, and she did it as if it were no more than a habit from birth. I did nothing, and when we were out on the landing and she stopped the engine, Fanny cried, 'Brilliant,' and Lelée said, 'Now we will need a lot of *essence* but I haven't got any money.'

I knew that it was my turn to do something and I said,

'I'll get some from Aunt Mimi, but how are we going to carry the stuff? Petrol is heavy.'

'We don't carry it. We will go with the boat to the pump in Villefranche, but you will have to ask Aunt Mimi if we can take the *pointu* there.'

'It's Clothilde you'll have to ask,' Fanny informed us. 'She'll decide.'

'Nevertheless,' I said, 'we will have to ask Aunt Mimi first.'

'Then it's better to be quick so we get to the pump before twelve o'clock when Benedict goes for lunch,' Lelée said.

We didn't have to get around Clothilde. When we told Aunt Mimi what we wanted she simply said, 'Clothilde. Go down to the *pointu* and see what you can do.'

That is when Clothilde had her say. 'You are going to make trouble for us with that *pointu*,' she said, and it was enough said. Thereafter she was more agile getting down the steps than I was.

Like Lelée, Clothilde's skill in manoeuvring the *pointu* seemed to have been bred into her from birth, even though she had been Aunt Mimi's housekeeper for almost half her life. But when she got us clear of the landing she handed over to Lelée who took us to the pump in Villefranche, and I shall never forget the joy of gliding across the Bay of Angels in that smooth and sea-loving boat, cutting through the sea so easily with its pointed bow and stern that it seemed to be gliding on stretched silk rather than water.

When Benedict, the *pompiste*, pumped the petrol into the *pointu* through a fine filter, he joked and teased Clothilde, and though we didn't understand all of it I guessed he was trying to find out what the four of us were doing with the *pointu*. Clothilde and Lelée treated him with contempt and though he gave them back as good as he was given it was Lelée who had the last word. She called to him as we pulled out into the bay, '*Crupeda Suzetta*,' which I counted as a feminine sort of pancake, but it didn't do justice to Benedict who was a huge man in baggy overalls, and with hands that were almost too thick to cope with money. Despite his provocative banter and his curiosity I decided that Benedict was, in fact, a friend of Lelée's.

But it was already a warning to us, because everybody who saw the odd wonderment of Clothilde and three children in that fisherman's *pointu* had to be curious, if not fascinated. Even I would begin to wonder why Aunt Mimi allowed us to use the *pointu* and why, in the end, she would also let us risk life and limb to recover Lelée's metal box. But the explanation was simple enough. It was Aunt Mimi herself. Nothing more than that needed explanation. Already she was as involved as we were, and I remembered my mother warning me: 'If Aunt Mimi gets her eye set on something, she will fix it and won't let go, so you watch out if that happens, because sometimes it gets to be a blind eye.'

CHAPTER 12

In fact it was Aunt Mimi who suggested the disguise of a picnic in the *pointu* two days later, and she organised it as if she were preparing a family outing on a pleasant summer's day. It was her idea to take us to some isolated little beach near the metal box and enjoy lunch, while Lelée went underwater to attach the box to the *pointu* so that at the end of the day we would pull it out of the rocks secretly and, if Lelée had her way, drag it back to the Boat House like a net full of fish.

Aunt Mimi didn't explain her picnic that way because the intention was obvious. All it needed was an isolated little beach near the box, approachable only from the sea, and private enough for us to spread ourselves. We knew where there was such a beach – in an inlet about fifty yards from the box, and that is where we headed.

'Better be a fish in the air than a woman in a boat.' I remembered that as we headed out along the coast – four females and one male. The attraction was not only Clothilde in her black apron and a big double hat – two straw hats in one – but there was also the imposing Aunt Mimi under a small 1930s parasol and wearing what I supposed was a stylish white Paris bathrobe over a swimming suit. Aunt Mimi, the immovable, in a swimming suit? It was almost beyond belief and yet I had seen her as agile as Clothilde coming down to the *pointu*, and I decided that all French women had secret bodies that only revealed themselves when you didn't expect it.

I shall never forget that picnic. The food which Clothilde and Aunt Mimi had prepared was in the best tradition of al fresco haute-cuisine, if there is such a thing. But first we had to land on that private little patch of pebbles, and even as we unloaded the picnic baskets we began looking around for the Silvios. They were not in sight. Nonetheless, we made a deliberate fuss of everything. We even had deck chairs for Aunt Mimi and Clothilde, and a big beach parasol. Then, when everything was spread out, Aunt Mimi decided to have a swim.

'You too,' she said to Fanny. 'You come with me and I will look after you.' Then she said to Lelée, 'Where is it?'

Lelée, who never liked Aunt Mimi taking charge, pointed to the spot near the cliff face where the box was. 'It's there somewhere.'

'Then Fanny and I will go there and see it,' Aunt Mimi said.

'You won't be able to see it,' I told her. 'It's too deep and it's hidden by the rocks.'

'Then we will go somewhere else and wait until you have captured it.' And she said to Lelée, 'You go and do what you have to do.' Then to Fanny, 'You come with me, and Beau can help Lelée.'

We watched Aunt Mimi take off her *bournous*, and without considering the rough pebbles underfoot, or the depth of the sea before her, she simply walked into it as if she were walking down the street. Fanny was already wearing her life-jacket and flippers, and she followed Aunt Mimi who swam off with huge overarm strokes that denounced the sea rather than embraced it. That left the sceptical, critical Clothilde to finish setting up the rest of the food taken from the baskets.

Meanwhile Lelée had been collecting a coil of rope as well as her mask and flippers from the *pointu*, and she said to me, 'Aunt Mimi is wrong. If we give the box to the Customs they will put me in prison for finding it because they said they would.'

'Don't you think she knows that?' I said.

'Then why is she saying such a thing?'

'She must have something else in mind,' I said.

'What else would she have in her mind?'

'How do I know?' I said impatiently. 'You can't ever tell with Aunt Mimi.'

Though she didn't understand our English it was Clothilde, spreading a tablecloth on the pebbles, who said, 'You are saying between yourselves what can you do with the box, so you are thinking of doing something else with it.'

'We're not thinking of anything,' I said. 'But if Aunt Mimi tells the Customs about it they'll arrest Lelée for finding it.'

'Then it is for Lelée to leave it where it is in the sea,' she said, undoing a bundle of *poussins* wrapped in grease-proof paper.

Lelée put the coil of rope over the side of the *pointu* and she told me to hold it afloat as she said to Clothilde, 'If we leave the box where it is the Silvios will soon find it.'

'Then make it disappear,' Clothilde said with her usual bad temper.

It was then that I decided that Clothilde knew what was really in the box, and she didn't like it. I suppose the look on my face gave me away because she said to me, 'You are a clever boy, M'sieur Beau, but you do not know everything, do you?'

'No, I don't,' I said. 'But do you know what's in that box, Clothilde?'

Lelée was far enough away from us not to hear Clothilde when she said to me, 'You make sure the Lelée doesn't do anything to make trouble for herself. You must look after her.'

In French it was more of an appeal than a command and I asked, 'How is she going to make trouble for herself? What are you saying?'

'Let her leave the box where it is or, better, she should hide it from everybody,' Clothilde said, and she raised the two roasted *poussins* in the air. Those elevated chickens, gripped in her fists, became her odd but powerful way of giving me responsibility for Lelée. In fact I knew how serious she was, and for the first time I began to think that Clothilde was right. There was some sort of danger for Lelée in that box, apart from the threat of the Silvios.

'Does Aunt Mimi know what is in it?' I asked softly.

'You will ask her, not me. It is her idea . . .' Clothilde said, and she walked off leaving me with that same curious puzzle about Aunt Mimi. Why was she allowing us, even helping us, to rescue the box? I accepted that, being Aunt Mimi, she wanted to know what was in it, but if the box was too big for money, what else could it be? I still wasn't sure that she knew, but with Aunt Mimi's own rules for her own untouchable behaviour I was sure there was some other reason why she was willing to let us find the box, even allowing for the hidden threat of the Silvios if they saw us. So I was thinking and thinking about it, and under Clothilde's powerful influence I was beginning to change sides. I was having doubts of my own about the box, although I didn't know what I could do about it. The problem was Lelée herself, and I was afraid that she was making a mistake.

But I couldn't desert Lelée. She was in the water, swinging the *pointu* around, and I too was in the water watching Aunt Mimi and Fanny holding onto a rock beyond the beach and laughing. When Lelée (already equipped to go under) relieved me of the rope, I said, 'Why don't you tell me what is in the box?'

She was still busy with the *pointu* and she said, 'My father didn't tell me what is in it. Soon we will see for ourselves, so why do you ask?'

'I don't know,' I said as I got into the boat, 'but I hope you know what you're doing.'

It was the best I could do, and my doubts were forgotten in the complicated business of playing off the *pointu* with a long line from its anchor. Lelée had put the coil of rope in the *pointu* at my feet and and I didn't know why she had given it to me in the first place. When I asked her she said, 'I wanted it wet so it doesn't tangle and will sink.' She had tied one end of it to the stern post and she told me to pay it out as she took the other end.

'But make sure it doesn't tangle as I go down,' she said.

'Is that all?'

'Yes, but you must also pay attention to the Silvios. If they come near and see us, then you must drop all the rope overboard and leave it.' As she went overboard herself I noticed that this time she was wearing the weight belt instead of carrying it.

We were under the cliff face and as she disappeared I fed her the rope, but I was also looking along the coast to see if there was any sign of the Silvios. Even with my glasses on there was no sign of them. Meantime, Aunt Mimi and Fanny had splashed alongside, and Fanny said, 'Help me up, Beau.'

'I can't,' I said. 'I have to keep the rope going.' I was still feeding it to Lelée, aware of the speed of her descent.

'Give me your mask and I will see for myself what she is doing,' Aunt Mimi said to me. 'And Fanny, you go back to Clothilde and help her, and watch for the intruders.'

By now the rope had gone slack and I knew Lelée had reached the box. She pulled the rope to get more slack and as I leaned overside and gave my goggles to Aunt Mimi, Lelée tightened the rope again and I realised that she was pulling herself up on it. She burst to the surface like a dolphin at sport and she was gasping for air as Aunt Mimi cried out, 'But that is bad for you, Lelée. You will damage yourself.'

When Lelée breathed deep and plunged again Aunt Mimi finally had my goggles on over her bathing cap and she had her head in the water as I kept a tight grip on the rope. I guessed that this time Lelée was tying it to the binding around the box, and when I felt the tug on it I knew she was on the way up again as Aunt Mimi called out, 'I didn't see her.'

'She's coming up now,' I said, and once again Lelée burst to the surface and took the usual huge gulps of air that now seemed to be her natural connection to the sea.

Aunt Mimi, gripping the side of the *pointu*, or rather the gunwale, shouted at her, 'You're not to do that again, Lelée.'

'It's done now,' Lelée said climbing into the *pointu*. 'So you start up the motor, Beau, and Madame Aunt Mimi must get out of the way of the propeller.'

'You are a very foolish girl,' Aunt Mimi said as she plunged off with her big arm strokes to join Fanny and Clothilde on the beach. 'I didn't know you suffered in the water like that.'

As usual, Lelée was dismissive. 'It's all right,' she said as I started the engine, and though I felt the *pointu* taking the strain, the boat didn't move. The jammed box was holding it back. I revved the engine even more and the *pointu* began to move as the box was shifting.

'It will come,' Lelée said. She was back in the water watching, but she suddenly lifted her head and said, 'Not so fast or the rope will break itself.'

I was pleased to be in action, pleased that Lelée had given me something responsible to do, but she shouted, 'It's not right,' and as I dropped the anchor she went under again. So I waited until I felt the strain as she obviously managed to twist the box to release it from some new restraint. When she came up she scrambled into the boat, pulled up the anchor and took over, giving the engine another burst as the *pointu* almost leapt forward with the liberated box behind it. But it jerked and bumped badly and I shouted, 'We've got to get it off the bottom.'

Lelée stopped the engine and together we heaved on the rope to raise the box, and even though it was lightened by the dense water I felt how heavy it really was. In fact when it was finally free of the bottom, the weight of

162

the box weighed down the stern. It was so heavy that I thought it must be filled with solid metal. But what sort of metal? Spare parts? Radios? I couldn't think of anything that would explain it.

'Now that you have captured it you must come and eat,' Aunt Mimi called to us. 'So leave it and hide it until it is time to go home.'

It was an order we obeyed, and as we anchored the boat and stepped from the bow to the beach, only Fanny had unadulterated joy for our achievement. 'You'll be a millionaire,' she said to Lelée, almost hugging her.

But Lelée pulled a tight face and said, 'Our Beau doesn't think so. Look at him. He is afraid of something.'

My face must have reflected my new concern and Fanny said, 'What's the matter, Beau?'

'Nothing,' I said.

Lelée laughed, a grim sort of laugh for her. 'He demands to know what is in the box,' she said. 'And now you are all in *tourment* about it because it isn't what you thought, is it?'

'No, it isn't,' I said. 'So what is in it, Lelée? Do you know?'

Lelée had taken off the top of her bikini and she was wringing it out. 'I don't know,' she said, 'but God will be great.'

I realised then that the contents of the box, whatever they were, had now become nothing more than a hope for Lelée, rather than the certainty of a box full of money. But I was diverted by Fanny saying to me, 'Turn around and don't look at her,' as Lelée took off the bottom of her bikini and wrung that bit out as well.

I made a mock gesture of covering my face as Aunt Mimi, wrapped in her robe said, 'What on earth are you doing?' to Lelée, but then she suddenly sat up in the deck chair and said, 'That must be the Silvios coming.' I turned and saw Mario and the Zodiac zooming by, not more than a hundred metres away.

They could obviously see us in our full glory. That is – our picnic. The parasol was up, the deck chairs were there, the food spread out on the tablecloth, and Clothilde was busy, while the three of us were a proper presence, with Aunt Mimi upright and important in her Paris *bournous*. It should have convinced them at a glance, but Mario swerved the Zodiac around in a big circle and came in closer to take a look. The twins were still in their aqualungs, and as they passed us they lifted their insulting hands to heaven in a mocking appeal and laughed and waved as they went off down the coast.

'Now we can eat Clothilde's repast,' Aunt Mimi said and it became an enjoyable picnic as we ate the combination of *cuou d'artichaur farci* (stuffed hearts of artichokes), *patano i bonis erbo* (potatoes fried with parsley), and *oeufs pochés* and *oeufs à la tripe* (poached eggs and eggs with tripe) with a small glass of wine each to soften its path. It was another meal I shall never forget and when it was over it seemed normal, despite the secret, expectant presence and pressure of the box, for Fanny and Lelée to continue their involvement in *A Captain at Fifteen*.

'How far have you got?' I asked them as they argued over the phrase 'a potential crew'. What sort of a crew was that? Lelée wanted to know.

'We're on page nine,' Fanny said. 'That's when Jack discovers the wreck.'

'But have you really understood what you are reading?' I asked her.

'Not some of the words or the meaning, but we understand enough and now it is exciting.'

It was the perfect answer as far as I was concerned, but as I lay back in the hot June sun, staring at the blue sky, I was more interested in what we were going to do with that heavy box when we got it to the Boat House. Nobody had mentioned the box over lunch, although we were all thinking of nothing else, and only when it was time to go did Lelée say to Clothilde and Aunt Mimi, 'You'll have to sit up in the front. Then the *pointu* will go better.'

We had not seen the Silvios again. Even so, as we loaded the *pointu* and as Clothilde sat silent and grim at the very prow of the boat, drying her feet, we were still watching for them. Lelée and I had, with a huge effort, raised the box off the bottom, and now that everybody was packed in I sat at the stern and Lelée took the engine and the wheel. We had raised the anchor and we began the manoeuvre that would decide how we got the box home.

'It's going to swing all over the place,' I shouted at Lelée as we left the little inlet. The box was beginning to veer from one side to the other.

'It will be better when we go faster,' Lelée said.

'You must tell me when it is going properly,' Aunt Mimi said, and it was only later that I knew why she said it.

When we picked up speed the box straightened out behind, but every time the smallest wave hit the *pointu* the box jerked, and I could see that the rope would break if we hit a big wave.

That was the situation when the Silvios arrived. They seemed to have come from nowhere, as always, but it was obviously from one of the inlets and, as they approached, Aunt Mimi cried out, 'You must go faster and faster, Lelée.'

Lelée's reply was to open up the engine even more, and as the Silvios came closer one of the twins shouted at us, 'You are stupid, unprintable women . . . what do you think you are doing?'

'We're going home,' I called back as nonchalantly as I could.

'You have picked up the box,' one of them shouted. 'Where are you hiding it?'

What happened next became a comic madness, except that it was serious and everybody was involved in it. When the yellow Zodiac came back, almost alongside, Lelée managed to swing the *pointu* around, not to avoid the Zodiac but to charge it. But when we almost rammed them, the twins were furious and, as if we were the aggressors, one of them shouted, 'Watch out, you blue-bottomed cretins . . .'

When the Zodiac splashed around and came back again Clothilde stood up and, rather like a mother angry with a

166

hopeless child, she shouted harsh Provençal reprimands at Mario who replied almost shamefacedly with Provençal insults, waving his arms. At the same time, Aunt Mimi was trying to pick up one of the long oars stowed on the side of the *pointu*, and Fanny too was trying to help, but she was obviously more hindrance than help.

'They don't know that we're pulling the box,' I said in a grim, loud whisper to Lelée. 'So what are they thinking of?'

'They think what they want to think, that we have it in the *pointu* under all that pile.' The pile was the towels, the picnic, the beach parasol, the chairs. And it was obvious by now that the twins not only intended to get the box, but they were going to get it by boarding us like pirates, so thereafter it became a noisy, shouting, give-and-take to keep them off. But even as Clothilde was attacking them, and Aunt Mimi was struggling to hit them with the oar, one of the twins, Enrico, managed to get his leg over the *pointu*'s gunwale as the two boats ploughed on, jammed together.

Clothilde was now at her best. She pulled off her hat and got a grip on Enrico's leg and tipped it overside as he shouted at her, 'What sort of an old unprintable butterfly are you? What do you think you are doing?' It was a language that even I could understand.

Then it became another example of feminine authority. Even as Aunt Mimi and Clothilde were casting off the legs and arms and bodies of the indignant twins, they in turn continued insulting the two women, this time calling them plucked chickens trying to be roosters. But in fact we were really in the hands of Lelée. She kept the *pointu* going at full speed, breaking away and swerving cleverly each time the Zodiac came back, which made it more difficult for me to go on hiding the rope as it trailed behind us. I tried to pull it in and release it so that it didn't stretch out, hoping that the Silvios wouldn't notice it in their conviction that the box was actually in the boat. So the real struggle for it went on between the twins and Lelée and the two women and even Fanny who used a wet towel to beat one or the other of the twins.

But it was soon obvious that we were losing the battle. Clothilde and Aunt Mimi couldn't keep unpeeling the vigorous assaults of the twins, and it got to the point where I had to forget the rope and intervene. I picked up the boat-hook lying on the floorboards and tried to push the Zodiac off, but Mario seized the other end of it, and in the tug-of-war I think he had finally guessed that the box was attached to the rope in the sea. Even as he began to shout something about it to the twins, Clothilde took the hook from both of us and plunged it into the bulbous stern of the rubber boat.

It was beautifully done, and Clothilde reminded me of Boadicea charging with her spear at the invading Saxons. But I shall never know if she intended to puncture the Zodiac or simply push it away. In any case the blow put a hole in the stern of the Zodiac and the effect was immediate. When air and water rushed into the hole she had made, the Zodiac's stern collapsed and the outboard simply roared to a stop. As the back of the Zodiac flooded it didn't sink, but it stopped dead and we ploughed on unburdened, enjoying the panic of our three adversaries who were trying to keep the Zodiac afloat as we left them.

But thereafter everything changed in the *pointu*. We now came forcefully and suddenly under Clothilde's orders and her first instruction, standing face-to-face with Lelée at the wheel, was to order her to head straight out to sea away from the coast.

When Lelée questioned Clothilde with that powerful French word, '*Pourquoi?*' Clothilde turned to Aunt Mimi and said, 'Why? It is, as I told you.'

Whatever Clothilde had told Aunt Mimi it had its effect. 'Go right away from the shore,' she told Lelée. 'You must go far out to sea.'

Resenting this new attempt to take all decision away from her, Lelée shouted, 'What for?' and it was obvious that she had no intention of obeying either of them.

'If you do not do it,' Clothilde said, 'I will tell M'sieur Beau to undo the rope and let the box go.'

This time Lelée was furious. 'What do you want me to do right out there? What are you saying?'

'Now you know about the box,' Clothilde told her, 'so take it out to sea, Lelée, or I will tell the *gendarmerie* about it myself.'

For a moment Lelée resisted, but I knew how powerful Clothilde's threats could be and when she said to me, 'M'sieur Beau, let the box go,' it was suddenly up to me again.

I wasn't sure what I should do. When I hesitated, Aunt Mimi said, 'Beau, do as Clothilde says.'

But Fanny wasn't having any of it. 'Don't do it, Beau. It's Lelée's box and she's got to keep it.'

In fact it was Lelée herself who saved me. She turned around to see if I was releasing the rope, but the best I could do in response was to shrug it off. It was enough to decide Lelée, who looked disdainful as she turned the *pointu* away from the shore and headed for the open sea.

This time I felt shamed, and I said to Clothilde, 'Why are you doing this to her?'

With her usual, measured temper Clothilde said, 'It is not a good question. Soon you will know yourself.'

So I asked Lelée at the top of my voice what it was all about.

'They are frightened,' she said.

'Of what?'

'The box isn't what it should be.'

'I know that, so what is in it?'

Lelée raised her hands and that was all I could get out of her.

In fact when Aunt Mimi had said 'head for the open sea' it might as well have been the horizon, and when Fanny said, 'It's not fair,' Lelée said, 'They are telling me to go all the way to Morocco.'

'You keep going,' Clothilde told her, and like that we ploughed on through the liquid sea until we were about two kilometres off Beaulieu and more than a kilometre from the curve of Cap Ferrat where Clothilde told Lelée to stop. Lelée cut the engine, and as the *pointu* slid gently to a stop, two fourteen-foot dinghies passed by, and somebody waved at us and laughed, otherwise we were alone in that wide-open jewel of the Midi – the sun already losing its ferocity, and the sky almost part of the sea itself.

The box at the end of the rope had dropped straight down under the boat and Clothilde said, 'Now stay here, and then let the box go.'

But Lelée would have none of it and said, 'No, no, no. I will bring it up. I want to know what was there for my father.'

Aunt Mimi had been sitting on the cushions in the bow and she said, 'Lelée, come here.'

Though Lelée was still defiant I wasn't surprised when she made her way to Aunt Mimi who said, 'You must listen to what Clothilde has to say.' And Clothilde said to her, 'You must do as I say, Lelée, because your father, the Corsairo, never knew that it was a parcel of arms in the box. It was not for him.'

A parcel of arms?

I had heard it but couldn't believe it. 'Is that what is in the box?' I said to Clothilde, and though my astonishment was nothing less than stunned amazement Clothilde ignored me and said to Lelée, 'We are not giving it up to the *gendarmes* because that would make it worse for your father and you and your mother. That is why we will leave it here in the depths where nobody will know where it is.'

But Lelée said grimly, 'You are always telling me what

171

to do, but what if there is more in it than a parcel of arms?'

I was such an outsider in this that I still couldn't understand their use of the French word '*tas*' as a 'parcel' for the arms. It was confusing, but whatever words they used I understood the extraordinary truth that the box contained smuggled arms, and when Lelée demanded angrily what sort of arms were in a box like that, Clothilde answered that they were *armes portatives*, *armes blanches* – small guns, portable guns. 'And if there is anything else, Lelée, you'll have to let it go. It is not for you.'

Clothilde and Lelée were face-to-face, almost steadying each other against the gentle motion of the *pointu*, and when Lelée said, 'But it was my father who was looking for it and wanted it,' Clothilde was adamant. 'Why are you saying that your father, the Corsairo, wanted the box? It was not for him. He was simply helping Mario who came that night to ask him, and the Corsairo didn't know it was meant for the Silvios. He would never make a contraband of arms for them.'

'You think you know everything about it,' Lelée said bitterly. 'But how do you know about my father?'

'Because, Lelée, the false wind of Mario came to see me yesterday and told me everything because he thinks the Silvios are so determined that they might do something savage, and he doesn't want that for you. So now I am telling you that it was not the Corsairo who wanted this box, and also Mario didn't tell him it was for the Silvios.' In her black apron and her restored double straw hat

Clothilde was a spectre over all of us, and she went on, 'There is nothing in that box for you, Lelée, so you do not want it.'

'But it's *my* box,' Lelée insisted.

It was Aunt Mimi who decided it when she said to Clothilde, 'Leave it for a little moment, Clothilde.' Then to Lelée she said, 'All right. You can pull it up if you can, and Beau will help.'

'It's foolish,' Clothilde said.

'I know it's foolish,' Aunt Mimi replied, 'but let her have it in her hand, then she will make up her own mind.'

The box was a dead weight when we began to haul it up, despite the density of the sea, and the only one among us who was delighted had to be Fanny who whispered to me as I was struggling with my part of the rope, 'Is it really full of guns and things?'

'That's what they say,' I told her.

'But what will Lelée do with them?' she whispered again.

'Ask her,' I said, and though I was both for-and-against Lelée I knew that a final decision was about to emerge from the sea. I realised too that Aunt Mimi had been thinking of Lelée – past, present and future – because there was something else embodied in the box that was, I suppose, Lelée's father. Above all, it had cost him his life. When we finally got it to the surface both Lelée and I were exhausted. We tied the rope to the stern post and the rowlocks which kept it half out of the water, weighing down the *pointu*, but it was finally revealed for what it was.

Its surface was more or less untouched by weed, being aluminium, but a sort of yellow slime of algae covered it so that it even looked sinister, and it was easy to see how well it had been sealed. The lid was attached to the sides with about ten little bolts, and the tarred binding around it had worn thin on the sharp edges of the box.

'Well then?' Clothilde demanded of Lelée,

Lelée waited. We all did, and nobody said anything. Then Lelée turned around to look up at Clothilde, and for the second time I saw the unwanted tears of the sun on her cheeks. Clothilde didn't say anything. She nodded at Lelée and with one of the sharp folding kitchen knives she kept in her thick apron, she cut the ropes and the box slid slowly out of sight, leaving a few bubbles of false air as it disappeared.

'That's not fair,' Fanny cried.

We all ignored her, and Lelée waited a moment as if she had to decide something. Then she stood up and said, 'I will go away from you now,' and she went to the stern and dived overboard.

When she came up she was already heading for Cap Ferrat which was more than a mile away. 'Now you can do everything you want without me,' she shouted over her shoulder as she finally disposed of us with the technique of a marathon swimmer who could swim forever.

Though we followed her, begging her to come aboard, Fanny appealing again and again, she ignored us, and it was only when we were a few yards from the Cap, still following, that I had an awful feeling that after this I would probably never see Lelée again. Though it was only a lonely, passing thought, I desperately wanted to call her back. In fact when she had plunged into the sea I had the feeling that she was deliberately going back to the sea, and we had lost her forever.

CHAPTER 13

But it wasn't quite like that. Lelée had not only abandoned us, she had simply disappeared, and though Fanny
and I went down to the Villefranche and Beaulieu beaches
searching for her, she wasn't there. Nor did Clothilde
know where she was. Nor was she with her mother at The
Spaniards. They had both disappeared, and nobody near
them knew where they were although two of the women
at the nets thought that the Rabo had gone to hospital and
Lelée had gone with her. But by now I felt that something
irreplaceable had gone out of our lives. Fanny was inconsolable. Then one morning, four days later, when Fanny
and I went down to the dinghy, we found it half sunk and

the outboard motor gone, and I knew that Lelée had done it to punish us.

Fanny refused to believe it. 'It was the Silvios that did it,' she insisted. 'That's the sort of thing they do, so it wasn't Lelée.'

'It was Lelée nonetheless,' I said, and when we reported it to Clothilde and Aunt Mimi (who were marinating something for dinner), Clothilde confirmed it. 'Lelée did it in the night. She was being wicked.'

'She isn't wicked,' Fanny protested, 'and even if she did do it then it's all your fault because everybody was so mean to her.' Fanny added this last attachment in English because we had been speaking French.

Garlic, coriander, hot peppers and other spices were being mixed with potatoes and fish in a big saucepan, and it was almost too much. The smell was delicious and Aunt Mimi said above its vivid air, 'We were mean to Lelée because there was nothing else we could do.' And she told us then that she and Clothilde had actually planned the picnic so that they would be there when Lelée retrieved the box. 'It was the only way that we could be sure to get our hands on it, so that we could take it out to sea and sink it.'

Disbelief had become part of my life, and here was another reason for it.

'But Lelée only wanted to bring it home and take what was hers,' Fanny protested. 'So why did you do it to her?'

Fanny's French was good enough now for Clothilde to say to her, 'If Lelée had taken the box away and brought it here, the Silvios would have come after her like wolves, and then what would have happened to her? It was better that Madame and I sank it where nobody could find it.'

'But if you already knew what was in it,' I said to Aunt Mimi, 'why didn't you tell Lelée what you were going to do?'

'Because Lelée is Lelée, and she would never have brought it up from the sea. She would have left it where it was and found some other way of getting it without us.'

What Aunt Mimi had said out at sea that day – that Lelée should see the box and make up her own mind – was beginning to fit into its proper place. It had always surprised me that she was so curious about the box. I remembered her need to inspect it underwater with my goggles on, and it seemed to confirm what she was telling me now, and I said to Aunt Mimi, 'Then it was all a trick from the very beginning.'

'Of course, and that is why Lelée has it in her mind now to punish us. For the Provençals revenge is always a bitter cry from the soul and Lelée is like that.'

'In that case the Silvios will want their own revenge,' I said.

'We will not let them,' Aunt Mimi said mysteriously.

By now I was feeling guilty about Lelée because I knew I had not been a loyal enough friend. I should have supported her, even though I knew she was wrong. Instead, I had simply shrugged myself out of it, so I understood why she was angry with me, even more than she was with Clothilde and Aunt Mimi. In fact only Fanny had defended her.

But there was more to come. That night, when Fanny and Clothilde had gone to bed, and Aunt Mimi was sitting in her favourite place at the head of the long table with her books and cuttings and the *Nice-Matin* spread around her, she said to me in her Aunt Mimi voice, 'I will explain to you what Clothilde did with the Silvios because you are ahead of your years, and because it is only Clothilde who could do what she had to do.' Aunt Mimi told me then that the day after we had raised the box and sunk it Clothilde had driven around the bay in the 2CV to inform her cousin Mario in no uncertain terms that it was she, not Lelée, who was responsible for dumping the box. 'She told Mario that it was her doing because she knew that the Silvio brothers were also *revanchards*, and would be planning an attack on Lelée. So they were not even to think of touching her, and as a threat to them Clothilde told Mario that she and I had written everything down about the twins and the box, and if they did anything to harm Lelée or the children or me or herself, all of it would go to the coastal *gendarmerie* in Fréjus and the criminal police in Nice.'

That should have been the end of the Silvios for us, but it wasn't quite the end. We ran into them once more, or rather they ran into us, but that was later, after Lelée came back.

She appeared one morning at breakfast and, ignoring Clothilde who was with us, and without making her usual sandwich she said, 'Today we will bale out the dinghy, and then we will go to Beaulieu.'

Relieved that she was back I was glad that I said nothing in reply, but Fanny was still upset and she said indignantly to Lelée, 'Where were you all this time?'

'Never mind about that,' Lelée replied and I knew then that she was not there to be pleasant to us.

'The dinghy is no good without the outboard,' I said to her, trying a compromise.

'I know all that, but tomorrow I will put it back.'

She left us then without any of her usual banter, and when Fanny and I joined her at the dinghy she was still being hostile. So Fanny asked her, 'Why did you want to sink the dinghy?'

Lelée didn't laugh as she normally would. 'Ask him,' she said. 'He knows everything.'

By now Fanny knew she couldn't overcome Lelée's attitude and she said, 'You don't like us any more, do you?'

'I don't like anyone any more,' Lelée replied.

'That's silly,' Fanny said.

If she was still angry with me Lelée was a faithful sister to Fanny and she said, 'Fanny-*fantoche*. You are silly and I am silly, but everybody else is stupid.'

I was beginning to be irritated with Lelée myself and I asked her cynically why she had only half sunk the dinghy. Why didn't she do it properly?

'I wanted to,' she said, 'but I could only tip it over enough to get some water in it. It got too heavy, so I could only half lift it and half fill it.'

'Well, it's going to take hours to bail it out,' I told her.

'You know everything, so what would you do about it?'

I was engineer enough to suggest getting the boat to the shore and then tipping it right over. Lelée didn't hesitate and we struggled to get the boat to the beach. I even managed to use some of my new-found strength to help Lelée. It was hot work, and when we had tipped it over and emptied out the water I plunged into the sea, while Fanny wiped the prow of the dinghy with her towel.

'We will go now,' Lelée said and she went up the steps to her *remorque* to get the bag of cloth, saying, 'It will be the end this time. There will be no more.'

I said, 'Where is the motor?' and she said, 'I will bring it, but today we will row.' And then she asked Fanny, 'Where is the book?'

'The book? It's upstairs. Why?'

'You go and get it,' Lelée told her.

'But we're ready to go.'

'You get it, *fantoche*,' Lelée said and though she had been ignoring me she told me to help her get the bag into the bow where it was driest. Thereafter we waited silently for Fanny to return, and in our silence I was beginning to appreciate just how much Lelée had been hurt. The rest of the morning was a repetition of the others when we laid out the cloth and spread the pieces and, finally, when the last one was sold Lelée said to Fanny, 'Now we will read.'

'I swear I didn't read a single word after you left,' Fanny told her. She produced the book from her own linen bag, and about now I realised that the one thing which had overcome everything else in Lelée's anger and revenge and absence was the need to go on reading *A Captain at Fifteen*. If the book had become a glimmer of light for Lelée, it had also become the only hope she had now to overcome the darkness that confused her.

I watched them as they began to quarrel about the page and the paragraph and the real sense of where they were in the book, with Lelée copying Fanny's favourite gesture of jabbing a finger on a word or a place, and I realised again how much I had missed Lelée's daily arrival at breakfast, her real daily presence, her provocation for anything she could tease me with, and finally I knew how much I would miss Lelée when we went home to England and left her here at the mercy of the sea which possessed her.

That is how it was when my mother arrived.

It was my mother who had given me the reputation of knowing everything because she was like that herself. She liked to be sure of what she said and did, and, like Aunt Mimi, she had her own rules for her own behaviour. She greeted Fanny and me at the Nice railway station with her own kind of embrace, and the moment she saw me she said, 'You are looking more like your father every day,' as if that was the most important thought to greet me with. And so it was, because the two of us had been her principal occupation for almost a year, and we had always been uppermost for her. Fanny had another niche because she needed no protection. In fact Fanny was simply there, without my mother having to worry about her, as if they had a mutual, unspoken understanding, although it was too often disturbed by Fanny's defiance.

It was now July and in those balmy days in the Midi you had only about six minutes to get out of the Train Bleu at Nice before it went on to Italy, but in that time my mother had captured a porter and descended with her luggage, and after our embrace she was already asking me, 'Did Aunt Mimi send Ibrahim with the car?'

Ibrahim was parked outside the station now, waiting, and my mother told me to go with the porter to Ibrahim and, after that, 'You can come back and Fanny and I will wait for you in the buffet because I need a brandy.'

I knew that she hated travelling, and that an overnight journey from London more than justified a rare glass of cognac, but I told her, 'Don't eat anything, Mama, because Clothilde has a proper breakfast waiting for you.'

'I'll have a coffee,' she answered and then, as if she had finally had time to inspect us, she said, 'You both look like Molinar sunflowers.'

'What's a Molinar sunflower?' Fanny asked, and though she had been unusually silent so far, she had a tight grip on my mother's hand which was also unusual for the independent Fanny.

'I don't know what they are,' my mother said, so I knew it was one of her inventions. 'But that's what you both look like.'

Everything seemed instantly normal now because we were used to my mother's casual inspirations and thereafter her dismissal of them. But I was wondering when she would notice that I wasn't wearing my spectacles and could walk almost normally. But I went with the luggage to Ibrahim, paid the porter from the money that Aunt Mimi had given me, and when I returned to the buffet she said, 'You can have a Perrier and then we'll go.'

I didn't want a mineral water but I would never reject anything my mother offered. In my long spell of helplessness she had, of necessity, provided me with the endless needs that were often difficult, so I had learned to accept everything I was given because I didn't want to make it more difficult for her by having any preferences. It had become a habit, and as we sat for a while in that old French State Railways' buffet, soaked in stale Gauloise smoke, bare with a tiled floor and plastic tables and cane chairs, it was almost the perfect place to see my unsentimental Breton mother after having been away from her for more than two months. In fact I was suddenly aware of the soft French lilt to her English, something I didn't notice at home.

'Why are you looking at me like that?' she asked as she caught my awareness. 'Do I look miserable?'

'No, Mama, you look English,' I said. I was teasing her because it wasn't true. My mother couldn't look anything but French. She was small, but small in her own French person; always rather alert in an abstracted sort of way, but always neat too, by nature rather than deliberately. Even at thirteen I could see what caring for my damaged father and me for almost a year had done to her. She was too young and attractive ever to look grim, but I could see the lines that had been forced on her lively face. She seemed to be thinking all the time of something elsewhere (a curious habit). But I knew what Fanny meant when she said to her, 'Beau's quite mad. You don't look English at all. You look like yourself, Mama, that's all.'

My mother laughed and that was always a reward. 'I know that,' she said, and Fanny was right in that too because there was something only of herself in her watchful face. 'I look like myself, but you do look *belle*,' she said to Fanny, 'and Beau does look *beau*, so I shall tell Aunt Mimi and Clothilde that they've done a miracle with both of you.'

Fanny was ready for that too and she said, 'It wasn't they who did it. It was Lelée . . .'

I had warned Fanny not to say anything about Lelée until Aunt Mimi and I could explain everything that had happened calmly, so I said to her, 'Later, Fan. Not now.'

'I was only trying to explain why you look so good,' Fanny said.

My mother shook us off. 'For the time being that will be enough.' It was her usual way of ending our disputes, and she said, 'It's time to go.'

Fanny's sudden attention to Lelée would be the course we would begin to take to our final link to the girl from the sea, because Fanny was now determined to persuade my mother to take Lelée home with us to London. So was I, although I knew that above all I would have to think of her mother and convince Lelée herself and overcome my own feeling that she would never leave her mother.

When we got to the Boat House, and when Aunt Mimi and Clothilde had made a modest French fuss of my mother and she of them ('You are like a couple of mush-rooms'), Fanny came close to Aunt Mimi and said softly, 'Now you can tell Mama about Lelée.'

'Not now,' Aunt Mimi said firmly. 'Your mother needs a rest.'

'Do you, Mama?'

'Yes, I do,' my mother said.

Then Clothilde said to Fanny, 'We will tell her every-thing when we tell her, so that's enough for now.'

'But you should tell her now. She won't be upset,' Fanny insisted.

'You will wait and you will see,' Clothilde told her, and because it was all said in French my mother was so impressed that she said to Fanny, 'I'm listening to your perfect English–French.'

'That's Clothilde's doing,' I said.

'No, it isn't. It's Lelée's,' Fanny argued.

'It's good enough,' my mother said as she left us, and thereafter we didn't see her for the next two days as she slept off her time, or she simply relaxed in the relief of French surroundings, in the soft embrace of the Midi air.

They became, in fact, two days of Lelée because she came every morning. But she seemed to come as a neces-sity. She was with us and not with us, and though it was breakfast time she wouldn't eat with us, and she wouldn't talk to Clothilde who took no notice of her. But I knew by now that Clothilde was the *extra-disciplinaire* and the guardian of Lelée whether she liked it or not. In the end it was Aunt Mimi who broke the first line of Lelée's anger when she told her on the third day at breakfast that she was behaving like a wicked child. 'You have punished us enough, Lelée, so now you are being shabby.' And this time Aunt Mimi used the word *mesquin* which could be used for being mean but it was Aunt Mimi's emphasis that made it more than that.

Lelée was sitting on the old stool which was normally reserved for Moucheur the cat. Lelée was dressed in what looked to me like a brief sheaf of pale yellow leaves, and replying to Aunt Mimi's sharp words she said, 'If I am wicked we will go now and paint the dinghy, so you will have to give me some money for the paint and that isn't being wicked.'

Lelée then made herself a sandwich and was eating it when my mother appeared. Though I was always aware of Lelée's perfections, I saw her that day and at that moment as my mother must have seen her, instantly mesmerised by the beauty of this golden girl. The pickled cucumber Lelée was eating so vigorously didn't matter, and I had to remind myself that Lelée was the same age as I was, thirteen, and when her first words to my mother were, 'Fanny-*fantoche* can't swim properly so I am going to teach her when we have finished the dinghy,' it seemed like a natural beginning for Lelée.

In reply, my mother said, 'You shouldn't eat pickled things for breakfast. They're bad for your skin,' and I knew then that they had made their own connections without any help from Fanny or me.

In those two absent days, when my mother was

resting and Clothilde had been taking cold snacks up to her, Clothilde had given us strict orders not to go near her. Now, at breakfast, Fanny said to her, 'Mama, you've got to tell Beau not to look when Lelée takes off her bikini.'

As she sat at the other end of the kitchen table and took the coffee and croissants from Clothilde, my mother said to me, 'Did you look at Lelée?'

'Not like that,' I said. 'Lelée just strips off when I'm there, that's all. She wrings out her bikini.'

'He shouldn't look,' Fanny said.

My mother turned to Lelée and said in a removed sort of way, 'Do you see him watching you?'

'Not when I'm doing what I always do,' Lelée replied.

My mother didn't seem bothered by it and said to Fanny, 'Is that what you were waiting to tell me about Lelée?'

'No, no,' Fanny said. 'They've got to tell you what happened with the *pointu* because Lelée is a smuggler and the Silvios chased us.'

'That's enough,' Aunt Mimi said. 'We will tell your mother all about it.' She had given Lelée the money for the paint, and as Lelée finished her baguette and her cucumber she said, 'I will go now with my *remorque* to Saint Jean for the paint, and you two can go back to the dinghy to finish the clean-up of the inside.'

It was said in Lelée's normal premonitory way but Fanny resisted it. 'If Aunt Mimi and Clothilde are going to explain what we did, then you should stay and listen.'

Then to my mother, 'The first thing the Silvios did was to try and sink us in the dinghy.'

'Fanny,' I threatened. 'Leave it to Aunt Mimi.'

'All right, all right,' she said.

My mother was aware enough not to get involved, and she told me to get the parasol and the deck chair and set them up on our beach. 'Can you carry them down?' she asked me.

'Beau can do everything for himself now,' Fanny said. 'That's what Lelée did for him. Anyway the *parasol* is in the *pointu*. We left it there when the Silvios attacked, but Lelée and I are going to stay right here and listen to what they say to you.'

'I don't need to know what they say to your mother,' Lelée said, 'so never mind about that.'

'Now you are being rude,' Aunt Mimi told her.

'I'm not being rude,' Lelée said. 'I am only saying what I have to say.'

'Well, even if you don't want to hear what they say about you,' Fanny said, 'I do.'

'Never mind that,' Lelée told her again. 'You go with Beau to finish the inside of the dinghy, and you do what your mother asks you to do with the parasol. Then you and Beau will get everything ready so that we will do the painting.'

Lelée took another pickled cucumber from the jar and left us, and though I was once again an outcast in this community of women, it was obvious that only Lelée had any authority here. So I obeyed, and I suppose that was the beginning of Lelée's conquest of my mother.

Pale as an English sky, my mother joined us at the dinghy and, lying on the deck-chair under the parasol, she watched us as we finished off what we were told to do – scrape away all the flaky paint from the floor planks. She was asleep when Lelée returned with the paint but she was half-awake as we began to paint the gunwales, and I wondered when her Breton rule for neatness – that good ships hate rough sailors – would reach Fanny as she sloshed paint with a reckless brush that would soon create a disaster. She said nothing because Lelée, watching over Fanny, was as strict with her as my mother would have been herself, and she enjoyed Lelée's resistance when Fanny wanted to know again what they had said in the kitchen and Lelée said again, 'Never mind that now.'

Silenced, Fanny got on with a more disciplined brush and thereafter it was the interruptions that arrested my mother when Lelée and Fanny took a break and tossed themselves again into *A Captain at Fifteen*.

Unfortunately my mother made the mistake of telling them that they should get on with the reading rather than waste time arguing about a word. 'But it's the words we are after,' Fanny pointed out. 'Isn't that right?' she said to Lelée.

It was an embarrassment for Lelée. 'It doesn't matter now,' she said to Fanny. 'We have finished, and we will go back to the dinghy.'

'But you don't have to stop,' my mother said to Lelée who was already escaping, and it was a first lesson for my

190

mother in the complicated problems of Lelée's complicated life.

In fact the next few days became a sort of mutual curiosity between them as Lelée and my mother sized each other up, and little by little Lelée took on my mother as she had taken on Fanny and me. Lelée was already concerned with my mother's exposure to the sun, and she told her, 'The oil you put on is not good for you in the sun. You must use the sea.' She insisted that my mother dip herself in the bay whenever she wanted to sit in the sun. 'Then you will be like me when the time comes.'

My mother replied with her quick laugh and one of her inventions. 'Only when the sun goes down, Lelée, will I look like you when the time comes because then nobody will see me.'

By now Fanny and I were feeling that we were getting somewhere, bringing them together, but Fanny, being Fanny, still had to know what Aunt Mimi and Clothilde had told her in the kitchen and she asked about it again when the three of us were alone that night.

'It doesn't matter what they told me,' my mother said. 'It was fortunate that Aunt Mimi and Clothilde were with you and could do what they did.'

'But weren't you angry when they told you what happened to Lelée?'

'It's too late to be angry now, Miss Fantoche.'

'What about the box the Silvios were trying to take away from her?'

'What about it?'

'What did Clothilde and Aunt Mimi say about that?'

'They said it must have been a ghost that Lelée was dragging up from the sea.'

Refusing to accept my mother's deliberate restraint, Fanny persisted. 'What did they tell you about the awful Silvios?'

'You were lucky that you had Clothilde to deal with them.'

'But we all dealt with them. It was a big fight. They were like pirates.'

'Clothilde said that you were very brave and you weren't frightened, so it doesn't matter now.'

'You're not going to tell me anything, are you?' Fanny finally protested.

'I am only telling you what you need to know, and now I understand why Lelée calls you a *fantoche*, because you are a little *fantoche*, aren't you?'

Adopting it so affectionately was as good as an embrace from my mother, and she didn't laugh when Fanny said, 'If Lelée says I am a *fantoche*, then that's what I am.' And though she went off to bed in a bit of a huff my mother said to me, 'Fanny has made of Lelée a protected species, but she is right about you, Beau, because Lelée is becoming more than a girl, so you must be very careful what you do.'

'What does that mean?' I said indignantly.

'You are still a boy, but Lelée is soon becoming a young woman, so you must remember she has her own peculiar problems.'

'You mean that she can't read?'

'Yes, but more than that. She told me yesterday that I must give you a little glass of wine to drink every day because you are old enough now to become more than you are.'

'Why would she say that?' I asked.

'I think she wants you to grow up a bit faster so that you can catch her up, but even so I think you're already well ahead of yourself.'

I accepted that as a fragment of my mother's silent sense of humour and I was flattered but aware that she and Lelée were looking for mutual answers to their feelings, even about me. 'Is that what you and Lelée talk about?' I asked her.

'Of course. Doesn't she call you M'sieur Beau?'

My mother was teasing me now the way Lelée did, so I gave up and in the end the main influence Lelée had on my mother was the obvious attachment she had for Fanny and vice-versa. When Lelée began teaching Fanny how to swim 'properly' it was Fanny's unquestioning obedience that surprised and pleased my mother. When Lelée made Fanny, unprotesting, hold her head under water with her eyes open, even before she started to swim, my mother asked Lelée what she was doing that for.

Lelée replied in French. 'It is so that the sea won't frighten her.'

Fanny was frightened of nothing but I saw the logic in it – knowing that the determined attempts by beginners

193

to keep their head above water usually made early swimming difficult. Thereafter Fanny seemed to spend more time with her head under the water than above it.

When my mother went for her own modest paddle in the sea (she was a poor swimmer – 'Bretons love the sea and hate the water'), Lelée did the same thing for her. 'You must do it like Fanny,' she said, and my mother unhesitatingly submitted herself, so that she too became a liberated head-down swimmer, and the two of them were now Lelée's legionnaires.

I was given another kind of treatment and it wasn't swimming. Rather, Lelée took me deeper and deeper underwater as we hunted the fish that Clothilde needed for her *soupe de poissons*. While we were plunging, my mother and Fanny sat in the dinghy fishing with rods because Lelée had made it their discipline. Like that, the three of us began to live with the sea, and I began to think it was Lelée's intention to soak us into it as if, like her, we wouldn't be able to escape it.

Except, of course, for their escape into *A Captain at Fifteen*, which the two of them were reading more effectively every day. Watching them, my mother said to me, as I lay on the pebbles reading Mistral's *Marianne*, 'They are like two thistles waiting for the wind to blow them away.' In fact it was my mother they now consulted when they wanted an explanation of a phrase or a word, and only when she wasn't sure did she say to them, 'Ask Beau, he knows everything.' So we were all in it, and I look back on those days as one of the happiest times in my life. By then, Fanny was convinced that it wouldn't be difficult persuading my mother to accept Lelée as an addition to the family in England.

But it had to end, and it did so in a curious sort of contradiction so that Lelée would lose something of the sea, and we would begin to lose something of Lelée. It began when Fanny wanted to take my mother to see the golden *merou*, now in the aquarium at Monaco, but she had to argue fiercely with Lelée who didn't want to go.

'But Mama does,' Fanny argued, 'so you have to come.'

'Not me,' Lelée said.

'Why not?'

'I don't want to see it,' Lelée said, and that should have been enough.

My mother suggested that at least Lelée could come along if we went in the *pointu*. 'You are the only one who knows how to handle it, Beau can't.'

Beau could, but I didn't argue and in the end Lelée agreed. But Aunt Mimi said, 'You can only use the *pointu* if Clothilde goes with you.'

The old give-and-take was again working between Lelée and Clothilde, so Clothilde was with us when we pulled into the mooring at the aquarium, and I was glad to see that though the *Calypso* had gone the *Espadon* was there. It meant that Didi could help us get into the aquarium the back way. He came out on deck when Clothilde called for him. Being a father of two daughters, and remembering the bold and talkative Fanny, he took her hand and we followed them into the aquarium the back way. I had forgotten that it would be full of tourists looking at the tanks filled with fish. Clothilde had remained in the *pointu* and my mother was listening again to Fanny's rush of French as she questioned Didi about the dolphins he and Falco had captured for the aquarium. I was behind them with Lelée who had come this far under protest and only to oblige my mother, but she stood back a little, while Didi tapped the glass of the big tank.

'Is that it?' my mother said, as suddenly and clearly a big *merou* emerged from one of the rocky ledges.

'That's not it,' Fanny said.

'That's it,' Didi said.

The golden *merou* was no longer a golden *merou*. It had turned grey, the colour of the tank it lived in, and when Lelée saw it I realised from the look on her face that whatever she had felt about imprisoning her wild fish, she had not anticipated that it would also lose its golden, glimmering beauty. Her jewel of the sea had been reduced to ashes. Now it was only a fish.

'But that's not fair,' Fanny protested.

As if it wanted to hide its shame, the *merou* turned and disappeared with a flash of its tail, but as it went we saw a little glimmer of gold, a small patch on its head, as it plunged into one of the fake caves.

'What happened to it?' my mother asked Lelée.

'I don't know,' Lelée said, 'because I am not a fish, am I, and never will be.'

It was Didi who explained that he and Cousteau had

thought the colour so unusual that it must have been a freakish but permanent fault in the scaly skin; but apparently it wasn't that at all. Its gold must have been the colouration the *merou* took on from its surroundings, so that there must have been a deep corner in the rocks near the Phare where the sun's rays had actually created a sort of golden cave where it lived, giving the *merou* its golden colour. Now it had lost its golden beauty in adapting itself to the grey mist of the aquarium.

It was such a surprise that we all waited for Lelée to say something, but she turned away and it was only when we were back in the *pointu* that I heard her say to Clothilde in a bitter undertone, 'We should have killed it ourselves and eaten it . . .'

Later on I would find all sorts of symbolism in that idea, but at the time I only saw Lelée responding angrily to the loss of something that was so much of herself and the sea that I don't think she could understand it, and when, on the way home, we encountered the Silvio brothers, they took the brunt of Lelée's wrath.

We were half way to the Pointe when, as usual, they appeared from nowhere (from Monaco in fact) and they arrived at full speed, zooming down on us with a huge swerve as if to envelop us. Again they almost swamped us with a wave of water but this time the *pointu* simply rocked because it was much bigger than the dinghy. When they came back Lelée abandoned the wheel to stand up and shout a litany of Provençal insults at them. They even drew alongside for a moment and she repeated the insults, but this time in French, and though I knew what some of them were, others were unknown to me and I suppose unmentionable, because even my mother protested to Lelée saying in French, 'You are not being yourself, Lelée, to use putrescences like that.'

In fact I thought Clothilde would reprimand her too, but Clothilde said nothing, as if she understood the reasons for the outburst. When Lelée returned to the wheel I knew that the loss of her golden fish would have a lasting effect on her.

With July as our limit, we were nearing the end of our stay with Aunt Mimi, and I knew that Lelée's bad language hadn't helped our cause with my mother, but it was quickly forgotten, because I think Lelée was so determined not ever to be a fish that she soon lost her misery. Thereafter we had some good picnics in the *pointu* so that everything was going very well, except that in the end the real problem we would have was not with Lelée, it came with the Rabo herself.

Clothilde and Lelée brought her to the Boat House one morning in her little Citroën 2CV, and even at first glance I saw that her condition had worsened. She had always been rake thin, but now her pale face under her Provençal headdress was nothing but bone and sinew, and she seemed to have shrunk to a child's size. But she was all alive, and when she spoke it was still the echo and manner of Lelée. The original was still intact, and she said to Aunt Mimi, who had settled her at the long table, 'I know that you were swimming with the children, but

Clothilde didn't swim with them and I think that's a pity.'
And then to my mother, 'Wouldn't you like to have seen
Clothilde in the sea with them?'

My mother didn't know if she should take it seriously
or as a joke, but she smiled in her sudden way and
responded seriously. 'I wasn't there that day, but even if
Clothilde didn't swim with them it doesn't really matter
because she is probably the best cook in the world, and
that's what the children love.'

It became then the sort of exchange that these like-
and-unlike mothers would enjoy, as if they had been
exchanging half-puzzling jokes all their lives. Or perhaps
they were meeting on common ground because they had
both lived in their own private world and would come out
of it only when their children were involved.

We were all seated around the table, except Lelée who
hovered behind her mother as if to guard her from anything and everything. But the Rabo was all there in body
and spirit, and she said to my mother, 'You do look like
your daughter, don't you, and she is like you too. But she
is a *garçonierro*, isn't she?'

'What does that mean?' Fanny demanded instantly.

The Rabo didn't answer. She simply laughed because
she had been teasing Fanny with a local Provençalism,
and it was Aunt Mimi who explained. 'It means you're
like a boy . . .'

'A tomboy,' my mother said.

'So I am,' Fanny said. 'Aren't I, Mama?'

'Nothing less,' my mother said, then to the Rabo, 'But

you are also a copy of your lovely daughter who is like morning dew from the sun. So we are lucky, aren't we? And she is a very brave girl.'

The Rabo looked up at her daughter and said, 'That comes from the Corsairo, her father, and because of the sea. But I want to tell you that she is not from the sea, because that is what you think of her, isn't it? But now she must leave the sea.'

She told Lelée then to open the linen bag which they had brought with them, and when Lelée and Clothilde had spread the contents out on the table we saw again the colour and beauty of the Rabo's offerings, not only square cloths and small bags, but even a little jacket. My mother already knew about the Rabo's work – it was all around us – but she was so impressed that she could only say, Oh no – her way of saying it was too much. Even Fanny was saying, 'Look, Mama, isn't it fabulous?'

'These are the things for you,' the Rabo said to my mother. 'This one will be your size because I want to talk to you about Lelée, but not with the children here, so you go away,' she said to Fanny and me, 'And thee . . .' she added in French to Lelée.

'It's not a good idea,' Lelée told her.

'It's good enough,' the Rabo insisted, 'because I must talk to Madame of the Beaumont family. But I will tell you afterwards what I say to her. You go away now and the rest of us will sit here and talk.'

Lelée obeyed and I knew why she did so. It was the same reason as my own – obeying my mother in almost everything so that I didn't make more trouble for her when she had trouble enough.

'You're not to take Mama home without me,' was Lelée's instruction to Clothilde as we left and went down to the beach where Lelée insisted that she and Fanny get on with their *A Captain at Fifteen*, but only after we had, under orders, soaked ourselves in the sea to protect our bodies against the sun. Though I had always watched them reading, this time I was amazed at how far they had gone into the book and how fast their reading went on. But my real thoughts were upstairs because I knew that the real problem for Fanny and me was what was being said between the Rabo and my mother in the dining room.

When Lelée took another plunge into the sea, as if that was part of the ritual of her life, Fanny said to me as I put down my Mistral, 'Did you ask Mama about Lelée?'

'No,' I said. 'In fact I was going to ask her today.'

'Why don't we tell Lelée about it?'

'Not now,' I said as I saw Lelée returning. 'Anyway,' I added quietly, 'I think I have left it too late.'

I didn't have time to explain that the Rabo was doing it anyway, but I was also remembering the way Lelée had hovered over her mother, and though I had been pushing it out of my mind I had no doubt any more that she would never leave her mother under any circumstances. That is what my mother said to me later that night when the others had all gone to bed. She told me how the Rabo had asked her to take Lelée with us to London, and had even offered all the money that Lelée had accumulated bargaining with foreigners on the beach.

'She said that Lelée must leave here,' my mother went on, 'because she wants someone to watch over her, to get her away from the sea so that she can somehow get an education without the sea's bad influence, and she says that you and Fanny are the brother and the sister who would always be there to look after her.'

'What did you say to all that?' I asked.

'I thought about it, as I always do, and I thought quickly for me, *Why shouldn't I take this beautiful girl with us?* But then . . .' She hesitated and I knew that she had probably reached the same conclusion as myself, and she went on, 'When I told the Rabo that Lelée would never desert her, she said with a curious laugh, a sort of mocking laugh at me and herself, she said, as she pulled off her headdress and I saw that all the hair had gone, "You can see now that it's not Lelée who will desert me, it is I who will be deserting her."'

'Does that mean she is dying?' I asked.

'I suppose so,' my mother replied, and it was so reluctantly and unhappily said that I knew how deeply affected she was, and she went on, 'When I asked Aunt Mimi about it later she said, "You never know with the Rabo because she will never give up." But Clothilde told me that the Rabo won't give up because of Lelée, and if Lelée goes away there would be nothing left for her. By then I knew that I could never even think of taking her away with us.'

'In that case we won't be taking her to England?' I said to be sure of it.

'But that's what I said, so why do you ask?'

'Because it was only today,' I told her, 'that Fanny and I were going to ask you to take Lelée with us, but I wanted to be sure it was hopeless.'

'I knew you were thinking like that,' my mother said, 'so now I can tell you that I would have taken Lelée with us because she is an *audacieuse* who would keep a good grip on me when I am becoming too much for you and your father. That is when I am not English, am I, nor is Lelée. She will never be like you and your father because you never, ever disagree or quarrel with me, no matter what I say or do.'

The only possible English answer to that was, 'But why should we quarrel with you?'

She made a despairing, hopeless gesture for both of us and said, 'Because I need a true *contraire* like Lelée and not just a childish one like Fanny.' She leaned close to me as if it were a confidence and said, 'I think you need one too, Beau, because it would be good for you to have a bossy big sister.' Now she laughed and I knew it was an unhappy laugh as well as a regretful one. 'In any case,' she went on, 'you and your father will never see Lelée as I do because I know that she is much more than a lovely girl. Then she said forcefully in French, *'Elle se maîtrise'* – I mean that Lelée will always conquer herself, like her mother, and if she ever came to us she would put something ringing like a bell into our quiet little English life

203

which has no bells in it at all.' She hesitated, but she was watching me very closely when she went on, 'I know you also wanted her to come, Beau, so I need you to understand why I had to say no to the Rabo. I could never have asked Lelée to desert her mother, could I? Can you understand that?'

'Of course I can,' I said, and because I knew how much my mother wanted me to understand and how difficult it must have been for her, I went on, 'But what did you manage to say to her?'

'I couldn't tell her anything that would hurt her,' she said, 'so I had to be careful not to give her the real reason. Instead I gave her all sorts of childish excuses about your father needing me, and running the house, and you, too, and other nonsensical things.'

'Do you think she believed you?'

'Of course she didn't. She knew that I was telling her a bowl of English lies, but she said in the same way that Lelée has of telling me what I ought to do – she just said, "You needn't worry about it because I know that if the time comes you will take her."'

Then my mother made a curious remark. 'I don't ever weep, do I, Beau?'

'I've never seen you weep for anything,' I said, and it was true. But I knew that my mother was making a confidant of me as she sometimes did when she wanted nobody else to know something, not even my father.

'I didn't weep for her, Beau, but I should have, and I did try because there is nothing else I can do for her. I know what the Rabo is suffering and it makes me very sad for the both of them, and I hope you are feeling sorry for me too because I can't do anything for them.'

I knew what she meant and I said, 'I know what you are going through, so you don't have to worry.'

'But you and Fanny will be disappointed.'

'Yes, but anyway I was thinking all the time that we couldn't take Lelée away from her mother.'

My mother sighed. It was rare, but it was usually a warning of something critical to come. 'You should have told me what you were thinking,' she said, 'but you are always like your father. Sometimes I have to guess if I want more from either of you. That's why I thank heaven sometimes for your *babillard* sister, although sometimes she is worse the other way. But I will say that it is such a pity about Lelée. She would have made it easier for me to get a better grip on Fanny too because they are already like peas in a pod, aren't they.' She was still watching me to see my reaction to her faith in me, but then she said, 'And what about this M'sieur Beau who never says anything to hurt anybody, and sometimes you don't say anything at all.'

'I didn't get the chance,' I told her, 'because haven't you said everything?'

'I know that. But I really do guess what you are thinking, and I'm quite grateful to the God above that you tell me as much as you do.'

My mother was teasing me now, and though she rarely kissed me, I was given the breath of her lips on the top of my head before I went off to bed. If I didn't kiss her back it was because my mother knew, as I knew, that we were a very close mother and son, although for me it was, as Mistral had said in his story of Marianne, 'Don't, thus, do more because more is often not enough.'

That is how it came to an end at Cap Ferrat. We never saw the Rabo again, and our last days at the Boat House became a sort of ritual of repeated, saddened regrets that it must end, but thereafter to consider the Boat House as our own, to return soon, even to stay forever. And that is how we severed our unbreakable attachment to Aunt Mimi and Clothilde, and to the daily bliss of their *Cuisinanero audio Provençalo*, their Cookery à la Provençal.

The two of them came to the Nice station to say their final Goodbyes, but Lelée didn't come. She had simply disappeared when I tried to persuade her to come and see us off. But as a last word she had said to me in a puzzled sort of way, 'Why do you always watch over me like that, and why do you *try* me all the time?'

'Don't you want me to?' I had asked her.

She had thought about it for a moment before saying, 'Yes, I do. I always want you to watch over me,' and that was my last attachment to the golden girl from the sea. In fact it was Fanny who was inconsolable, particularly when Lelée had already refused to keep *A Captain at*

Fifteen. Instead she told Fanny to take it home and read it for her. 'It's finished for me, Fanny-*fantoche*,' she said. 'It's all over now.'

Fanny, clinging to her little sea-horse necklace, wept, and I told her that she shouldn't weep because, with us going away, it was for Lelée like the loss of another golden *merou* and she would get over it. In fact I only half-believed this myself. But we were already missing her. Even in her absence she was there among us as we stood together with Aunt Mimi and Clothilde waiting for the train and all we could manage were more sad farewells to that perfect summer – to the lyrical perfection Lelée had made of the emerald sea and the burning gold of the Midi sun, high above the hills.

And so we returned, after two days travelling, to our sea-less, horizonless London. A week later we could still feel some of the aftermath of the Bay of Angels, but a month later it was all gone when, physically restored, I was back at school, my father had returned, and Fanny was back to normal, arguing day-to-day, hour-to-hour. Once again we were a family under the authority of my unsentimental mother who stood over us like a master mariner commanding a crew that needed a firm hand, so that life returned to the proper, ordered, sensible temper of an early autumn's English earth and English sky.

That is, until the winter, on a Saturday morning, when the front-door bell rang. As I opened it to a wet and gloomy day I knew, even at a glance, that once again my life was about to be turned upside down.

Lelée, more beautiful than ever, was standing calmly in the rain, dressed thinly in a cheap print frock and rejecting outright any need to shiver, as if she was already defying the challenge of this cold, English world of big differences. She was saying to me, even as I opened the door, 'You'll have to get all my bags and boxes from the street because the taxi driver wouldn't bring them in. So you go and get them before someone steals them, and I'll go inside and tell your mother that I'm here.'

Obedient to the commands of this future engineer of anything and everything, I did as I was told, and so began another kind of adventure with Lelée that would continue but never replace the recollections of those halcyon days at Cap Ferrat. But that is another story which some day I will have to tell, though only as a curious and unpredictable postscript to this record of the golden girl who came into my English life from the seductive depths of the deep, blue sea.

Also by James Aldridge

The True Story of Lilli Stubeck

When the down and out Stubeck family arrived in St Helen no one expected that they would stay for long; nor, when they left, that it would be without their daughter Lilli.

It was a mystery, too, why wealthy Miss Dalgleish should 'buy' the wilful girl and try to tame her, for Lilli was fiercely determined never to be anyone but Lilli.

With a battle of wills for possession of her soul, and with the unexpected return of her scavenging family, what did the real future hold for Lilli?

Winner of the 1985 Children's Book Council of Australia Book of the Year Award.

Also by James Aldridge

The True Story of Spit MacPhee

The people of St Helen are concerned for young Spit MacPhee. Spit lives a hand-to-mouth existence with his eccentric grandfather, Fyfe MacPhee, in an old shanty on the banks of the Murray River.

When old Fyfe dies, Spit finds himself the subject of a dramatic court case which polarises the religious and moral attitudes of a typical Australian country town in the 1930s. Yet, such is the strength of young Spit's character that, when the truth about his life with his grandfather is revealed, no one is left unchanged.

Winner of the 1987 Guardian Children's Fiction Award. Winner of the New South Wales Premier's Literary Award. A major television series starring Sir John Mills.

Come exploring at

www.penguin.com.au

and

www.puffin.com.au

for

Author and illustrator profiles

Book extracts

Reviews

Competitions

Activities, games and puzzles

Advice for budding authors

Tips for parents

Teacher resources